SLEIGH SPELLS

Winter Witches of Holiday Haven

BELLA FALLS

Evermore Press

Winter Witches Books by Bella Falls

Sleigh Spells

Cheery Charms

Merry Mischief

Enjoy the whole Winter Witches of Holiday Haven Series!

SLEIGH SPELLS

Hark! The Herald

Volume No. 352 — Editor Archer Olsen — December 18, 2020

Rudolph Missing! Jack Frost wanted for questioning in connection to the reindeer-napping.

All of Holiday Haven and the North Pole are on the lookout for the missing reindeer. Police say to be alert for a shiny red nose. Some have even said it glows. All of the other reindeer are highly concerned and want their front runner returned safely. Citizens worry about toy delivery delays without Rudolph to light the way. Will Santa be able to see his way through a snow storm without Rudolph and his mighty nasal superpower? Experts say it's unlikely. If you have any information on Rudolph's location or Jack Frost's whereabouts, inform your local police.

Is Christmas Canceled? Heinous Hex stops toy production at Toy Workshop.

Who could be behind the dastardly deed? Who in all of Holiday Haven and the North Pole would want to keep toys from reaching all the good girls and boys in the world? Children full of questions for Santa. If not enough toys can be produced in time for Christmas, how will it be determined who gets toys? Some kind of points system? Santa could not be reached for comment.

Murder rocks the Christmas Market! Cursed cocoa linked to illegal potions ring.

Trouble at the Holiday Haven Inn? Mishaps and magical mayhem threaten to disrupt five-year anniversary celebration.

Santa's Sleigh Stolen: Is Christmas in jeopardy? Workshop security baffled and elves in disarray!

Introduction

Have yourself a very Merry Witchmas in Holiday Haven, where the magic and mystery of Christmas is *snow* joke!

Aurora Hart hates everything Christmas, but how could she turn down the opportunity to serve one year of probation in Holiday Haven versus a full sentence for her crimes? Saddled with a talking squirrel roommate, Aurora is doing her best to keep a low profile as she bides her time. Everything is going fine ... until Santa's sleigh gets stolen.

Now, all eyes are on her and the other town Humbugs, and it's up to Aurora to keep her behind from ending up back in jail. With the help of a very important person from the North Pole, she finds herself hot on the trail of the real culprit. But it will take her having to do something she's never done before—accepting new friends and their assistance. Only then will Aurora be able to turn not only her own life around but also Christmas for the entire world!

Will Aurora be able to solve the mystery of who stole Santa's sleigh in time? Or will the culprit get the final *sleigh*?

Grab your cup of cocoa, sit in a comfy chair by the cozy fire, and find out now in *Sleigh Spells*! And be sure to check out the other magical mysteries of the **Winter Witches of Holiday Haven series**!

Preface

There's one special place where mistletoe and holly
Are hung up all year to make everything jolly
Where sharing good cheer is never a toll
Because every day's Christmas in the North Pole

Visit Holiday Haven, where our Winter Witches
Will share their own stories to keep you in stitches.
They all have some magic and mayhem for you
With a dash of adventures and mysteries, too.

Will Christmas be cancelled without Santa's sleigh?
Or without any toys to be given away?
What happened to Rudolph or the impish Jack Frost?
Without them, will the entire holiday be lost?

Will cursed cocoa take all of the merriment away?
Will a missing magical wishing box ruin the day?
Find out what happens in each single story
And enjoy the shared world in all of its glory.

Come to Holiday Haven, the special place where
We hope you enjoy all the magic we share.
From all of us cheery Winter Witches, we say
Have a bright Merry Christmas and a Happy Holiday!

Chapter One

Aloud banging noise interrupted my fitful slumber. Annoyed, I rolled over and pulled the covers over my head, burrowing under the cave of blankets. The pounding became more insistent with every second that passed, but I refused to give up my cocoon of warmth. Man, I missed winter in the South. At least then, I didn't risk freezing my patootie off every second of my existence.

The door to my room creaked open and something scuttled across the floor. A light figure bounded on top of the mattress and bounced up and down my bundled body.

"Get. Up. Get. Up. Get. Up," the squeaky voice chirped at me with every spring as he jumped.

I groaned in response. Peeling back the quilt covering my head, I saw the silhouette of my roommate outlined by the light shining through the crack in the door.

"Just five more minutes," I begged, pulling the blankets back over my head.

My tiny roommate scampered up my chest and grabbed the quilt from my fingers. "Hey, hey," he said, rapping his little knuckles on my bared forehead. "You need to get up. The probation officer is here to check on you."

I brushed his touch away and tightened my fingers around the blankets in defense. "I don't wanna," I whined. "It's way too early. I'll bet it's still dark outside."

"Yeah, yeah," the squirrel squeaked, jumping up and down on my torso. His bushy red tail twitched in agitation. "But I don't want them here any longer than they have to be, know what I mean?"

Giving in with a groaning yawn, I threw the covers off and sat up. "What did you steal this time, Nutty?" I asked my squirrel roommate, who scrambled back and squatted in my lap.

"Didn't steal. Found some nuts that needed a new home." His beady eyes darted left and right, checking to make sure nobody else could hear him.

"And would that new home be inside your tummy?" I pressed a finger into his little potbelly of a stomach.

Instead of laughing like the little doughboy did on those television commercials, he flicked his tail in annoyance. "Doesn't matter. Just need the fuzz to go away as quick as possible. Okay, gotta go clock in at my job. Good luck with whatever new one you get assigned to today. Try not to burn the place down." With a little twitch of his whiskers, my roommate bounded off the bed and scampered out the door.

It wasn't my first time dealing with the police, magical or mortal, and I doubted it would be the last time. Retrieving my hoodie from the floor where I'd thrown it last night, I put it on and zipped it up over my pajama top. No clock was needed to know that the officer had chosen an earlier hour than necessary to do the probation check on purpose. I hated when those at the top tried too hard to assert their authority.

Trudging out of my room in my flannel pajamas, I stuffed my hands in the hoodie pockets, ready to face the consequences of my uncontrolled magic. The probation officer waited just inside the doorway to our small abode, the snow from his boots melting all over our doormat with a cartoon snowman on it that said *Frost Impressions Last*. He tugged off his mittens and pulled the bulky hood of his coat off his head to reveal silver hair woven into braids on either side of *her* head.

"Oh," I exclaimed, my surprise melting away some of my surly attitude.

The officer chuckled. "Not who you were expecting, huh?" she said, stuffing her knit gloves into the pockets of her jacket and wiping her feet on the doormat. "I get that a lot. May I come in?"

Her politeness threw me off, and I fumbled in my reply. "Uh, sure. I mean, I guess you can do what you want since I don't own the place."

The female officer smiled at me. "Still, it's your home." She struggled out of her bulky coat and looked for a place to put it.

I pointed at the coat hooks by the door, and she hung it up next to mine. It took her a couple of seconds to unwrap a red-and-green scarf from around her neck. By the time she took off all her cold-weather accoutrement, she was left wearing a red-and-black plaid flannel shirt over a green turtleneck, a pair of well-worn jeans, and her boots. If I hadn't seen her in her more official coat, I would have thought she was just a friendly neighbor stopping by. Except I didn't have any friends. And no one ever stopped by.

The woman clapped her hands together as she surveyed the small space. "It's a little chilly in here." She blew on her hands to warm them up.

I shrugged. "It always is. Can't seem to get the heat to work right."

Nutty didn't mind the colder environment since his

furry coat kept him warm enough. And I'd learned to wear as many layers as possible. Since the squirrel and I were given the free accommodations to live in, who was I to complain?

"But you're a witch. Surely, you could cast a temperature spell," the officer challenged.

I scoffed and shook my head. "Guess you didn't read my entire file. My magic is..." *Broken*, I admitted to myself, unable to say the words out loud.

"Oh, I read the file on Aurora Hart just fine." The officer walked around the small living room, checking out the bare furnishings. "But I figure it only tells a small part of your story. I want to know more about *you*, Rory."

I narrowed my eyes at the stranger. Instead of playing the tough authority figure, wanting to scare me straight, she chose to try and be my friend. Neither tactic ever worked, so I chose to give her as little as possible and kept my mouth shut.

The officer stopped her snooping and stood in front of the cold fireplace. "You should at least be able to cast a warming fire," she challenged.

"Sure." I made my way over to her, grabbed the nearby box of matches, and struck one, throwing the flame into the pile of logs. A plume of smoke wavered above the wood until the fire crackled to life. "There."

The officer watched me as I set the box of matches on the mantel. "You don't trust yourself," she stated.

"If you've read my file, then you don't have to go back too far to find out why," I said, staring at the dancing flames in the fireplace to keep the officer from seeing my frustrations. "You're here to assign me to my third job, not try to fix my life, Officer..."

"Noelle," she finished in a soft voice. She reached out and touched my arm. "You've only been here for two weeks. It may take longer to find the right fit for you, but I promise, we'll do our best."

Her kindness melted some of my icy shield, and a little hope leaked into my chest. Unable to handle being disappointed yet again, I yanked out of the woman's hold. "Whatever," I mumbled.

Instead of berating me for my insolence, the officer sighed. "I get why trust doesn't come easy for you. But if you would give this place a chance, maybe you could stop running long enough to discover who you are and what you can do."

She flourished her hands in the air, and the scent of pine trees, smoke, and a hint of cinnamon whirled around us. The temperature of the room increased by a few degrees, and I warmed up enough to unzip my hoodie.

"Neat trick," I admitted.

"I can teach it to you if you want," she offered. "It shouldn't be that hard for you to master since you possess fire magic."

I snorted. "You make it sound so simple, and yet we both know it's not. Because that's not my only dominant power." Taking a big risk, I held out my right hand and concentrated.

Water pooled in my palm until I had enough. With great effort, I forced the liquid into a familiar shape until my magic froze it into its form.

"A key. Interesting choice," Officer Noelle said.

"It's the only thing I ever learned enough to control, thanks to the one witch who took me in for a little while as I was growing up. You can imagine all the uses for keys he made me create." The fog of self-loathing and doubt that followed me since that period of my life filled me to the brim. "But he dumped me when my fire magic misfired and set off an alarm that got us caught. First and only time I was glad my powers didn't work just right."

Instead of telling me how worthless I was or how much I

belonged behind bars, the officer moved closer to me. Her eyes flashed so light blue that they reminded me of the ice in my hand. "Our past doesn't have to dictate our future. Sure, you've been in trouble before. I hope in Holiday Haven, you can choose a different path."

My mouth opened and closed like a fish out of water. I couldn't think of any sarcastic response to give her, so I showed her the rest of why it didn't matter where I went in the world. Because wherever I was, trouble followed.

I held up my left hand next to my right and let the ice key tumble into it. With considerable concentration, my fire energy heated the object until it melted and evaporated into steam. "Fire and ice," I sneered, ignoring the trickle of sweat rolling down the side of my face. "Not a great combination at the best of times, let alone inside a witch who can't control either power."

"Rory—"

"No," I interrupted. "Just ask the boss at the wrapping factory. I got frustrated while trying to tie some ribbon around a box and ended up setting some of the paper on fire. Or talk to Lumi at the reindeer sanctuary, where I almost hurt one of the reindeer by freezing its hooves in a block of ice! Without control, I'm a danger to those around me. I thought serving my time here would keep others safe. Instead this place is full of more people I can hurt." My chest heaved and my panting breath echoed in the small room.

Officer Noelle dared to smile at me. "You have no idea how special you really are, do you? To have two powerful elemental magics exist inside you—that could only happen in someone who was strong enough to master both."

"Yeah, I feel really special," I scoffed, staring at my hands. "Maybe I would have been better off serving the entire five-year sentence in jail."

"But you took the deal. And here you are in your very own

house," the officer said, ushering me over to the tiny living room. Choosing one of the two rickety wooden chairs from the small dining table, she dragged it over in front of the couch.

"Not alone," I countered, slumping onto the lumpy cushion. "But Nutty's not the worst companion to have around."

She laughed out loud, and for the first time, I noticed the lines of age around her eyes. "No, he isn't. Even if he gets a little too tempted once in a while by his addiction." Glancing behind her at the squirrel's room, she kept chuckling and shaking her head. "Nutty's already extended his time here by two extra months with his shenanigans."

I couldn't help but smile. Never in my life would I have guessed I would end up with a squirrel for a roommate. At the same time, Nutty was about the only good thing in Holiday Haven so far.

"Do you mind if I fix a hot drink before going back out there?" she asked, nodding at the door. "A little warm-up might do us both good."

Before I could answer, she waved her hand in the space between us, and sparkling snowflakes swirled in the air until two steaming mugs manifested on the coffee table. I peeked into my drink, ready to refuse it since I hated cocoa, which seemed to be the only beverage available in the whole town. Who needed so much sweet? I liked my hot drinks just like my life had been up to this point—bitter with nothing good added in.

A familiar scent hit my nose, and I breathed it in with relish. "Is that...coffee?"

"Black like you like it," Officer Noelle replied, picking up her mug and sipping on it with a smug smirk.

My mouth gaped, but I stared at her in suspicion. "Who are you?"

"Someone who wants to see you succeed," she answered, concentrating on her drink and giving me no other clues.

I picked up the mug and took a tentative taste. My eyes rolled in the back of my head at the bitter goodness. "Oh, sweet Santa, I've missed this."

The officer guffawed at my reaction enough to spill a little cocoa. She wiped her wet fingers on her pants. "Well, you better drink it all because you're gonna need the strength to handle the next job I'm sending you on."

The temporary good mood the coffee gave me waned. "Where?"

Instead of telling me outright, she dug in her pocket and pulled out a folded piece of paper. "Be there at ten." She finished the rest of the contents of her mug and smacked her lips in satisfaction, licking off her cocoa mustache.

I read the address a couple of times. "What business is this?"

Officer Noelle stood up from the rickety chair and considered my question as she made her way to the coat hangers by the door. "I think it's better if you find out for yourself. That way, you won't worry about all the ways you might mess things up before you even try."

"Too late," I mumbled under my breath as she wrapped the bulky scarf around her neck.

She grabbed her coat and stuffed her arms in the sleeves. "Oh, and Rory, do your absolute best at this job. There aren't an infinite amount of opportunities for you, and I'd like to see you keep one for more than a week."

"So would I," I said, jumping to my feet to open the door for her. "But I can't help but be worried it will all go badly all over again."

The officer hesitated in putting on her mittens. She stuffed them back in her coat pockets and held my hands in hers. Warm tingles spread across my skin, running up and down my arms.

With her intense eyes gazing into mine, she spoke low. "If you expect the worst, then that's all that you'll get." She placed my left hand on top of my right hand, and a strange energy pulsed against my palms. "Perhaps changing the way you approach life will open more doors for you. Give you new opportunities."

Officer Noelle released my hands with a wink. With caution, I lifted my left hand away and gasped at what I found. A perfect rose blossom of ice sat in my palm, its crystal petals sparkling.

"How did you do that?" I whispered, cradling the precious creation with great care.

The officer chuckled as she pulled her mittens on. "The magic was all yours. I just gave it a little nudge."

I shook my head in denial, but deep down, I wanted her words to be true more than anything else. "How?"

Officer Noelle placed a kind hand on my shoulder. "First step is to accept where you are and figure out how to make the best of it. And then you have to fully accept who you are. Do that and you might have a chance to be surprised at what you can accomplish." She opened the door, and a blast of frigid air burst inside.

I shielded my eyes from the whirl of snow that followed. When I recovered and blinked, the kind officer was nowhere in sight. Her disappearance left me with more questions and very little time left to pull myself together and get to my new job.

Chapter Two

I stood in the middle of the bustling street, clutching the piece of paper with the address that Officer Noelle had given me. My awkward position forced a few people to have to walk around me, but my absolute shock kept me from caring too much.

The timber of the storefront was painted a dark green, matching the color of the window frame upstairs. Above the door in bright red and gold letters was painted *Yuletide Yummies*. Tinny holiday music floated down from some unseen speakers above.

Not exactly sure what type of yummies the store sold, I shuffled closer to the nearest display window and shielded my eyes to see inside. Every ounce of space was jam-packed full of holiday scenes built from baked goods. Gingerbread structures rose out of a field of shredded coconut snow, and it took me a second to recognize the loose interpretation of the center of Holiday Haven.

Icing dripped off the scalloped rooftops mimicking icicles. Someone had taken a lot of time to pipe in all of the details to showcase every single store on the main street. Of course, Yuletide Yummies was the star of the entire display with its tiny windows lit up from the inside. I crouched down for further inspection and saw a minuscule version of the exact display in the window of the gingerbread replica.

The door to the store opened, and a sweet scent filtered out onto the sidewalk.

"You've got to be kidding me," I muttered to myself. "Who goes to this much trouble?"

A tinkling titter assaulted my ears, and a honeyed voice answered my question. "That would be me, Wren Warbler, owner of this store and baker extraordinaire!"

I stopped gawking at the window and stood up straight to find a grinning woman at least an inch or two taller than me, smiling for all the world like I was her best friend. Her peppered hair was piled up into an elaborate bun on the back of her head. Curled tendrils fell around her face, but they seemed more deliberate than happenstance. A pristine apron hung around her neck and tied at her waist displayed an embroidered store logo but not one speck of flour. Odd for a baker.

Despite my hesitance about my new place of employment, I forced a smile and introduced myself to my new boss. "Oh, I was just admiring the work that went into the display. I'm Aurora Hart, and I guess I'm your new employee."

The warm grin on the owner's face melted. She grabbed me by my arm and dragged me to the corner of the block of storefronts. "Help comes through the back door, not the front. I'll meet you there." She pointed once for emphasis and turned away from me, her frown disappearing as she greeted other potential customers standing in front of her store windows.

I chuckled ruefully to myself as I obeyed her edict. Throughout my life, I'd run into all different types of bosses at the numerous jobs I'd started—and lost. My relatively short time on probation in Holiday Haven continued that sad tradition. Both the supervisor at the wrapping factory and Lumi at the reindeer sanctuary had been incredible in their attempts to integrate me into their businesses without much drama. It had been my mistakes that had forced me to leave. If this Wren Warbler wanted to scare me straight on my very first day, she'd have to try a lot harder.

Somehow, the owner got to the back of her store before I did. She stood in the doorframe, beckoning me to hurry inside by snapping her fingers. Glancing around the small parking lot at the back to make sure nobody else had seen my entry, she closed the door behind us. The earlier warmth she'd displayed when first we met was long gone.

I stood inside a large kitchen at the center of a flurry of activity. Small elves that came up to my waist bustled around, and one of them carrying a large sack of flour bounced off the back of my legs. The bag dropped on the floor with a dull thud.

Wren yanked on my arm to pull me aside. "You'll need to make sure when you're back here that you stay out of the way," she warned me, glaring at the offending elf with disapproval. He mumbled an apology to both of us, picked up the sack, and scurried away.

There were at least six others working at different stations around the kitchen. Some sprinkled ingredients into an industrial mixer. Another couple switched between rolling dough out on the marble counter and cutting out different patterns.

"That's Flake and Flippy at the mixer with Buttons being the clumsier one that ran into you," the owner pointed at each one. "Pepper and Ginger are in charge of making more gingerbread cookies. Depending on the design cut out, we can turn those into pretty much anything."

I waited for her to introduce me to them but realized her lack of intentions. I cleared my throat. "I really like the new trend of ugly holiday sweaters," I said, remembering the single treat I'd bought myself after last Christmas when I'd found one stale cookie on sale.

Wren blinked at me. "What trend?"

"You know, where the cookie is in the shape of a sweater and icing is used to make it look like all those heinous sweaters with bold designs like Christmas trees or reindeers," I explained. When she still seemed perplexed, I kept pushing, filling the awkward silence. "People will have parties just so they can wear these sweaters. Not that I've been to one, but I heard about them."

One of the elves sitting on a stool at the counter busy with her decorating job giggled, and Wren shot her an unpleasant glance, sniffing in dismissal. "I don't see why anyone would think any sweater with Christmas decorations it is ugly, but then again, it has been an age and a half since I've visited the outside world."

She ushered me through a different door and up a skinny staircase into a bare room with cubbyholes on the wall. "This is where you can put your belongings at the beginning of the day. Although considering your background, perhaps you shouldn't be here," she finished on a whisper, as if not saying the words out loud would be less offensive.

It took great effort to maintain my cool. The last thing I needed was to get upset and either spark a fire or freeze one of her elves into an ice block. Taking a deep breath to calm myself, I forced a smile on my face. "If you know my circumstances, then you should know the terms which I am bound by."

Wren's lips pursed as she thought about it. "Still...perhaps I should limit your actions until I am certain whether this arrangement will work out."

I huffed a little. "I've worked a register before and am perfectly capable of serving customers."

Her eyes widened in horror. "Oh, no. You will definitely not be dealing with any of the money." Once she heard her own knee-jerk reaction, she attempted to recover and placed a hand on my arm. "No offense."

I allowed her touch even though it didn't feel particularly reassuring. "Well, I've never baked before, so not sure how much help I could be in the kitchen," I admitted with a shrug.

She actually cackled at my silly assumptions. "Oh, I would never trust you with my recipes."

I tilted my head. "Then I'm sorry, but I'm not sure what else there would be for me to do."

Light footsteps on the stairs interrupted us. The same employee who'd laughed at my ugly Christmas sweater cookie explanation entered. She stood several inches taller than the others even though she only reached the height of my elbows.

"Ms. Wren, I couldn't help but overhear you. I have an idea," she offered in a quiet voice.

The owner sighed. "What's that, Vale?"

"Well, you wanted me to man the stall at the Christmas market for the afternoon. Why doesn't..." she paused for me to give my name.

"Aurora," I said, pointing at my chest.

She grinned at me. "Why doesn't Aurora help me for today? It would be nice to have the help and the company."

Wren considered the idea, her eyes flitting back and forth from her employee to me. "I suppose," she acquiesced with a frown. "But if you're going to represent Yuletide Yummies, then you'll need to wear something much more festive and a lot less...drab." Her finger plucked the string of my dark hoodie underneath my black leather jacket.

Not wanting to have to be assigned to yet another job, I

quickly divested myself of my leather coat. Unzipping my favorite piece of clothing, I shrugged out of the hoodie as well. "No problem, although if we're gonna be running around outside, I'll need something to keep me warm."

Wren's left eyebrow crooked up. "It should be easy for you to cast a heating charm to do the trick, but I might have something else for you."

The owner walked over to a closet and retrieved a large garment. She held the fabric up in front of me to check its size. "There. That should do it."

I stared at the monstrosity. "I can't wear that," I complained, frowning at the gingerbread man costume.

The corner of Wren's mouth crooked up in cruel amusement. "If you're going to be representing us, then I want you to do it right. See our logo on the cookie's apron?"

"Oh, everybody will know who's responsible for me wearing that," I said, backing away from the costume. "Surely you have something else I can wear. A real apron perhaps?"

"If you're going down to our stall at the market, then this is what you have to wear," Wren insisted, shaking the brown fabric at me. "Or you can go home and wait for another job opportunity, which might be hard for *you* to find once I let it leak that you were difficult to work with."

Vale widened her eyes in a plea for me to agree. Gritting my teeth, I gave in. "Fine. Give it here."

Wren's mood lightened as she got her way. "Excellent. You may change in here and then help Vale load up the sled to take down to the market. Hand out samples of the Kringle Cakes, peppermint brownies, and...fruitcake."

The taller elf wrinkled her nose. "Oh, not the fruitcake."

Wren's mouth curved into a disapproving scowl. "I will be entering it as the store's bakery entry for the Seasonal Spirit Awards this year. It would be nice to get some support from the people prior to the voting."

To avoid whatever disagreement those two had, I encouraged them to leave so I could change. The costume zipped up over my existing outfit, and I immediately missed my hoodie. Avoiding the mirror by the door at all costs to keep from loathing myself, I stomped down the stairs and endured the snickers and giggles at my expense.

"That'll do for now," the owner said, failing to suppress an expression of malicious glee. She handed me a handwritten list. "Here, I've written down some things I'd like you to say when you're handing out the samples."

I took the paper from her and read her scribbled handwriting. "'Your *presents* is requested at Yuletide Yummies. *Yule* be sorry if you miss out on the goodies from Yuletide Yummies. Treat yo'*elf* to Yuletide Yummies.'"

The taller elf covered her mouth with her hand, but her shoulders shook from her giggles. It felt right to stick my tongue out at her, so I did like the brat that I was.

Wren cleared her throat to stop our shenanigans. "Vale, make sure you stay with Aurora the whole time today, especially when she comes back to change. Do not let her out of your sight," she warned, turning to gather her things.

My anger got the best of me, and a little flame shot out of my fingers and scorched the floor. I stomped my boot again and again to make sure I didn't catch the entire place on fire.

The owner stopped in her tracks. "What was all that commotion?"

"Nothing," I insisted, pasting the fakest of fake smiles on my face.

Instead of leaving right away, she narrowed her eyes, scrutinizing me. "Vale, I'll be dropping off the order to Carol at the Holiday Haven Inn, so you won't have to do that."

"Thank you, Ms. Wren," the smaller girl said, keeping her eyes down.

Just as she began to gather her things to leave, Wren

paused. "And make sure those charity folks selling their sad little sugar cookies are nowhere near our stall at the market."

"But they're selling them for a good cause," Vale defended. "The reindeer sanctuary can use all the help we can give them."

I had really liked Lumi and what she did with the retired reindeer. It had broken my heart to have to quit because of my own stupid magic. "Perhaps we could donate some of the proceeds from today's sales," my mouth suggested before my brain caught up.

Wren narrowed her eyes at me and took a step closer. "How dare you suggest taking money away from *my* business."

Vale slid in front of me. "You know, having others witness you donating generously might help sway their favoritism your way."

The bakery owner bit her red-lipsticked lower lip. "Maybe you're right. Let's make it...one percent of whatever we make from the market. I'll make sure everyone knows who the money is from when I present the check to the charity."

"Yes, Ms. Wren," her underling replied, moving to stand beside me.

The owner grabbed her coat and purse off of the coat rack with such haughty force, she almost knocked it down. "I'll be back in time for the Spirit committee meeting tonight. It would be highly advisable for you to be in attendance. Toodles," she sang out.

Vale observed my outfit for the first time, and she surveyed my torture. "I would tell you to change back, but the chances that one of her minions would tattle on you is too high. I don't want to get you in trouble on your first day."

"Me neither," I agreed, glad to find someone on my side for a change. "Better to endure a little humiliation."

I ignored the snickers from the other elves as I helped the friendlier one load up some containers with individually wrapped baked goods. We carried each large box outside the back door and hefted them onto the front of a sled with red metal runners gleaming underneath.

"All that's missing is a mess of dogs to drag it for us," I said, breathing in the cool air. I kept my surprise at how warm the costume was to myself.

Vale chuckled. "We don't need any." With a little flourish of her fingers, the sled slid forward on its own.

"I'm still getting used to the different types of magic around here," I said, walking beside the diminutive woman.

Vale looked up at me. "I'm surprised a witch like you could be caught off guard."

"If you're referring to my crooked past, then you might be sad to know that for the most part, I've never really been around a whole lot of magic," I said, keeping my gaze on the ground. "I kinda fell through all kinds of systems of life, mortal or magic. I'm far from normal on either spectrum."

Without hesitation, Vale took my hand in hers and held it as we walked down the street. "I know all about being a bit of a misfit. Try being half elf and half witch when you live in a district of the North Pole. I've always felt a little out of place."

Most of the time, I shied away from touch, compassionate or otherwise. But something about the half elf's genuine kindness broke through some of my barriers, and I took advantage of the comfort she offered. It even helped when others snickered at my costume as we ventured down the street towards the stalls for the outdoor market.

When we reached the market, I stopped walking and stared up at the towering tree erected at the far side. "Whoa," I exclaimed.

"I know," Vale agreed. "I think it's the biggest one we've had yet. Besides the usual basic trimmings, each citizen of the town places an ornament on the branches to give it a more personal touch."

"That sounds...like a nice tradition," I finished, uncomfortable about my usual lack of Christmas spirit.

She leaned into me a little. "Maybe you can hang an ornament of your own sometime."

I let out a quiet grunt, not wanting to scare her away with my past nor let myself get bogged down in it either. Breathing in the crisp air, I asked her to point me in the right direction. We wove our way down a row until we found a stall whose tent color matched the storefront of Yuletide Yummies with the same logo painted on it.

Vale busied herself arranging the different baked goods on the table while I stacked the boxes behind the table to make it easy to find the items. I knocked over one of the containers, and it flipped open. A few of the wrapped goodies spilled out, and I rushed to put them back in until I noticed their difference.

"Vale, what are these?" I asked, holding up a cellophane bag with a red-and-white ribbon tied at the top.

"Oops, pretend you didn't see those," she said, rushing over and snatching the bag out of my hand. "Ms. Wren would be upset if she saw these mixed in with her baked goods, but I promised to bring them for a few people."

I examined the box of extras. "Did you make them or something?"

Vale blushed. "Yes. I'll admit, baking isn't exactly my passion. Chocolate and candy are." She untied the ribbon and offered me what lay inside. "Here, try one."

Although I didn't prefer sweets, I refused to hurt her feelings. Taking one of the dark brown treats with dark pink stripes, I stuffed it in my mouth.

The second I bit through the chocolate, I moaned in delight. "Holiday hexes, that's so good," I mumbled, trying not to chew with my mouth open. "That might be the best thing I've ever tasted."

Vale's cheeks darkened from light pink to bright red like Rudolph's nose. "Thanks," she whispered.

"I'm not kidding," I reassured her. "And I'm a tough customer since I typically don't like anything sweet. But this is like the perfect combination of a little bitterness plus the tartness of some sort of fruit."

"It's a dark chocolate and raspberry truffle," she explained, closing the bag and tying the ribbon around the top again. "You might as well keep this bag for yourself."

I glanced down at my silly costume and patted it all over. "Where would I put it?"

We both giggled at my predicament. She placed the bag by the sled. "You can have more when we're done here. But first, we've got to get you out there so you can have a first good day at work." Vale picked up the loaded tray of samples to hand to me.

I accepted the platter but hesitated. "Do I really have to say all those things our boss wrote down?"

My cohort widened her eyes in shock. "What, you think you can't ho-ho-handle it?"

With a groan, I rolled my eyes. "Not you, too."

Vale pushed me from behind out the back of the tent. For such a short lady, she had a lot of strength. "Come on, you can do it. I believe in you."

As soon as I exited our stall, I stood for a moment in the shining sun. Not once in all my life had anybody said those words to me with such sincerity. It took me a second to tamp down the wave of emotions rising inside of me. With a big sniff, I took on the challenge of being someone worthy of her faith.

Moseying through the crowd in my ridiculous costume, it didn't escape my notice how a little bit of happiness filled my heart and squeezed out my usually morose mood. It became easier and easier not to wince when repeating the silly puns to advertise Yuletide Yummies as the day progressed.

I had to return several times to the tent to reload samples of the other two baked goods—but never more fruitcake. And each time, Vale made sure to keep my spirits up with encouragement and kind words.

At the end of the day, I returned to the store stall, and exhaustion settled over me. I rubbed my jaw. "I swear, I don't think I've ever forced myself to smile as much as I have today."

Vale counted up the money she'd collected, pulling out a small amount and setting it aside. "I hope at least one of those smiles was genuine. Did you have a good day?"

I gave her question some thought. "You know, it wasn't half bad." I set the tray of leftover samples down. "Except I couldn't get rid of all of the fruitcake. And I really tried."

The smaller woman picked up one of the sample squares and popped it in her mouth. "There," she said through her full mouth. "That's at least one less piece. And believe me, Ms. Wren will definitely count all the leftovers."

Without hesitating, I popped one in my mouth. The second I bit into the thick cake, I regretted it. It took me several chews to get to the point where I could talk. "She wants to enter this into some contest?"

Vale swallowed her bite with a grimace. "The Seasonal Spirit Awards. They're an annual event, and each of the towns that make up the entire district of the North Pole compete to see who has the most spirit."

"And she thinks her fruitcake will win?" I asked, accepting a gulp of offered cocoa to wash down the last of my bite. All the flavors combined caused me to shiver in disgust.

"Oh, Wren Warbler takes the SSAs very seriously," Vale

exclaimed with wide eyes. "She's been the head of Holiday Haven's committee for several years now."

"Has the town ever won?" I asked, helping to load the last of the containers on the sled.

Vale sighed. "Not once. We've come close, but that's not good enough for Ms. Wren. She's determined for our town to win this year. Once you're around her long enough, you'll see how scary she can get about it. If I were you, I would avoid tonight's SSA meeting."

"Oh, I doubt she'd want me there anyway." Considering how the owner of the bakery had reacted to my current probational status, I didn't think she'd like a known criminal to take part in whatever she was in charge of.

The shorter girl picked up the bag of chocolates from wherever she'd stashed it and handed it to me. "You've definitely earned these. I hope you like them."

Wanting to get rid of the fruitcake and cocoa taste in my mouth, I unwrapped the crinkly package and picked out one of the truffles. I moaned in absolute pleasure. "Not that I'm an expert, but I think these are fantastic. Why are you working at the bakery and not in your own shop? If that's just a sample of your talents, then I'll bet you'd have tons of customers lined up for your chocolates."

"Renting space costs money, and I've almost got enough saved to qualify for a loan," she said, her brows furrowing. "Mama and Papa offered to help, but this is something that's all mine. I wanted to do this on my own."

I tipped my head to the side. "I get that."

"I've been saving every penny from working at Yuletide Yummies, but Ms. Wren keeps me so busy that it's hard to find the energy at the end of the day to work on my own stuff," Vale confessed. "I've been half wondering if I should ask her to sell some of my stuff on commission rather than trying for my own place."

"And let her take some of your profits?" I scoffed, wondering if the haughty owner would try to take the credit for the delicious candies, too.

She shrugged and pushed the sleigh out of the back of the tent. "At least it would be something. And maybe she could help me build my reputation. But thanks for the compliment. It's nice to have someone believe in my work."

"Ditto," I declared, offering her a sincere grin.

Vale handed me the stack of money she'd kept off to the side. "Come on, Aurora. You can help me donate this for the reindeer sanctuary."

"I'd be happy to." A warm sensation spread throughout my body, and I reveled in the unfamiliar but welcomed glow. "And Vale?"

The half elf stopped walking and looked up at me. "Yes?"

"My friends call me Rory."

Her face brightened with genuine joy. "Excellent. Let's go, Rory."

Chapter Three

The best thing to come out of my first week at Yuletide Yummies was a friendship with Vale and the fact that I hadn't lost the job...yet. Because Christmas was fast approaching, the hustle and bustle of the market kept both of us busy and out of the bakery almost every day. Except today.

When I arrived, I found the kitchen devolved into a mass of chaos. I almost got knocked over by Buttons again as he scurried around the kitchen carrying ingredients. Instead of the usual elves manning the mixer, Wren stood over the industrial machine, supervising every ingredient going into it.

"Everything has to be perfect," she shouted. "Today is not the day to mess anything up."

"Why?" I asked, stepping out of the way of Pepper carrying a tray of cookies fresh out of the oven.

Wren gawked at me as if I'd grown a second head from my neck. "Santa's sleigh. It's arriving today to help kick off the beginning of the Seasonal Spirit Awards."

I snickered at the thought of everyone getting excited

about a simple sleigh until I felt the weight of everyone in the kitchen staring at me with disapproval.

"It's a big event that we all look forward to. And it's the reason you're getting a free afternoon off, missy," the owner scolded. "You would be best to respect our traditions if you want to fit in at all."

The door from the front of the store swung open with a bang, and Vale entered the kitchen with a frantic expression. "Clarence over at the pub just called. With the increase of traffic today, he wants to add to his typical order for more mince pies, plum puddings, and shortbread cookies."

Wren stopped monitoring the mixer. "Well, he should have thought of that before the last moment." She shook her head before returning to her position of control. "I swear, I would think a vampire who's been around as long as he has would know better."

"There's a vampire living in the North Pole?" I asked in total confusion.

Vale waved at me. "Several, actually. All types of supernatural beings are welcome to live and work here. But Clarence runs Whet Your Wassail at the end of the next block. It's a typical British pub with all the usual fixings. Plus, he brews some really good beer."

"Does he call it Holid-*ale*?" I joked.

Several of the elves snickered, and Wren cleared her throat to get everyone back on task. "Could we please stay focused? With the big arrival today, we're going to be busier than Santa on Christmas Eve."

"Actually, that's the other reason I came back here. I'm getting slammed up front. Can Rory help me?" the half elf asked.

The owner scowled at her employee over the glasses set at the end of her nose. "Who's Rory?"

"That's me." I raised my hand and waved it at her.

Wren looked me up and down. "If it were any other day, I wouldn't allow it. But since we've got to sell as much as possible before we close down for the big event, then I don't really have a choice. Change out of your dour clothes and wear one of the clean aprons."

I bounded up the stairs to the room above, happy to shed my leather jacket and black hoodie as long as I didn't have to wear another silly costume. Rushing back down to join Vale, I skirted the edges of the kitchen and pushed my way through the swinging door to the front.

A large group of customers crowded the place, and a line extended from the counter almost out the door. All eyes fell on me, and I ignored the heat rising in my cheeks from all the extra attention.

"Rory, thank goodness," Vale exclaimed, handing me a white box. "Fill this with four snowballs, a hot chocolate, and a half a dozen of the Santa's hats."

Panic froze me in place. "I don't know what any of those things are."

My friend reassured me with a quick grin. "Here, I'll show you." She pointed at all the different trays of goods. "These cookies dusted with powdered sugar are the snowballs. The hot chocolate isn't a drink—it's a dark chocolate brownie with a little chili to spice it up and a toasted marshmallow topping. And these are cheesecake bites."

Using some tongs, I picked one up. "Oh, I get it! The strawberry on top with the whipped frosting around the edge makes it look like Santa's hat."

It took me several orders to figure out the names of all the baked goodies, but I finally hit my stride, glad to be able to do something that didn't require my humiliation and wouldn't result in my magic going haywire.

When we came to a lull in customers, Vale pulled out several empty trays from the display case. "I'll go get more and bring them out. Do you think you can handle things on your own?"

I flexed my hands, hoping my magic wouldn't misfire under pressure. "Sure."

The bells hanging from the door jingled, and a tall man with brown hair and the greenest eyes I'd ever seen walked in. My breath caught at the sight of him, and his eyes flashed to mine as if he heard me. A different kind of heat rose in my cheeks, and I picked up a nearby towel to wipe down the top of the counter. My entire being hummed in awareness of his slow approach, but I kept my gaze down.

The man stood for a quiet moment at the front, watching my manic cleaning of a few crumbs. When I dared to glance up at him, he smiled, and it took considerable effort to keep my legs from shaking.

"Hey there," his deep voice rumbled. "I don't think I've ever met you before." He stuck out his large hand. "I'm Wyatt."

My mouth opened but no sound came out. I attempted to shake his hand but realized I was wearing gloves to serve the food. Jerking my hand away, I knocked over the stand of flyers with this month's specials on them. They scattered all over the floor.

Flustered, I drew in a deep breath and walked around the edge of the counter. The nice guy was already picking some of them up, and I crouched down to retrieve the rest. When I stood up, he handed the sheets of paper back to me, and his fingers brushed over mine. A crackle of energy pulsed between us, and I yanked away from him, afraid I was about to ruin the moment by burning or freezing him.

"Rory," I spit out, clutching the flyers to my chest. "I mean, Aurora. My name is Aurora." I blew a strand of hair out of my face.

Instead of backing away from the crazy lady in front of

him, Wyatt stood his ground. The corners of his perfect lips curled up. "Well, which is it?"

I got lost focusing on his Southern gentleman accent and manners as well as how my fingers longed to run through his hair and play with the curls at the nape of his neck and missed his question until he chuckled.

"Hmm? Which is what?"

"Is your name Rory or Aurora?" he clarified.

My cheeks flamed, and I scooted around the counter again to put a little distance between me and Mr. McHottie so my brain could function. "Aurora. My name's Aurora. Hart," I finished while stacking the flyers back together.

He tapped his finger over the left side of his chest. "As in heart?"

"No *E*," I explained.

His grin widened. "Ah, like a deer, then."

The bells on the door tinkled again, and an older woman wearing a bulky coat with a matching hat and scarf entered. When she caught sight of me talking to Wyatt, she winked and busied herself with browsing.

"It's nice to meet you, Aurora Hart," the man said, his accent growing just a little deeper. "Looks like you've already done a lot of business today." He tapped the glass of the display case.

"Oh, there's definitely more coming out." I glanced back at the swinging door, wishing for Vale to return with more stuff to give the guy more choices.

"That's okay, what I want is right here." Wyatt stepped a little closer.

My mouth dropped open again, and I failed to find anything to say. My flirt was definitely broken...if it ever existed in the first place.

With an expression that mixed mirth with trouble, he

tapped his finger on the front of the case. "I'll definitely take a bear claw."

It took me a second to gather my wits. "Oh, right. You want one of the pastries." I snatched a clean pair of tongs and a piece of parchment paper from the shelf beside me.

He chuckled, and the rumble of it reverberated through me. "Unless there's something else you're offering?"

Leaning down, I slid the back of the case open. "Which one's a bear claw?"

Wyatt crouched down and gazed at me through the window. He pointed at the second shelf. "Those there."

I chose the largest one with the most glaze dripping off of it and placed it in a paper bag. Standing straight again, I asked, "Anything else for you?"

He opened his mouth to say something, but Vale interrupted us when she bumped the swinging door open and dragged a cart with several loaded trays behind her.

"Oh, hey Wyatt!" she exclaimed with glee when she caught sight of the man at the counter. "I see you've met my friend Rory."

His left eyebrow raised. "So, it's Rory, is it?"

I experienced yet another level of embarrassment heating my cheeks. "Only close friends call me that," I uttered, handing him the bag.

Wyatt handed me some money. "Then maybe someday I'll earn that privilege. It's good to see you, Vale. Will I be seeing you again soon?"

"You going to see Santa's sleigh today?" she asked as she refilled the display case with baked goods.

He shook his head. "You know where I'll be. Why don't you stop by afterwards? And bring your *friend* so I can get to know her better." With a quick wink, he took his leave.

I watched him exit, admiring his backside, still a little flustered. The other customer finally approached the counter, cackling. "Don't worry, honey. There are plenty of us in town who think Wyatt Berenger's a tall drink of water. If I were several decades younger and not totally in love with my husband, I might have made some moves on that hunk myself."

Vale stopped restocking the shelves. "Ooh, are you interested in Wyatt? I could totally see you two together." She clapped her hands together with enthusiasm.

I looked between the two ladies, unable to express the mix of emotions roiling inside of me. "I'm gonna go take a break," I declared and hightailed it out of there.

When I entered the kitchen, I found most of the other employees gone. Wren stood at the mixer alone with her back to me. She must not have heard me enter, so I crept around the sides towards the staircase, keeping an eye on her.

Just when I made it to the first step, I witnessed the owner pull out a small pouch from her pocket. She opened it and slipped her hand inside. After a brief moment, she pulled out some of the contents and sprinkled them into the batter she was mixing. I leaned forward to try to find out what she was adding, but the change in my weight caused the first stair to creak, and she jolted at my presence.

"Oh, I didn't hear you come in," Wren said, closing the pouch and stuffing it back into her pocket.

I held up my hands, a bad habit from all the times I'd been caught doing something I wasn't supposed to. "I didn't mean to intrude. I was just going to take a break. Where's everybody else?"

"We're done with most of the baking today, so I told them they could go ahead and head to the town square for the big event early," she replied. "I'll be closing down the front of the shop in about an hour. We'll sell what we have left out there and call it a day."

"Sounds good." Instead of bolting up the stairs, I changed

my mind about taking a break and headed back out to join Vale.

I couldn't get what I'd just seen out of my head. What in the world was Wren adding to her mixture?

After telling my friend we only had an hour left, I tried to find a moment to tell her about what I saw, but the number of customers increased until we sold out of every cookie, cake, and bear claw. Even though Vale and I were left alone after she locked the front door, we still had to clean up everything and get things ready for the next day. We got so busy that I forgot about my question until we both entered the kitchen to finish up.

Wren placed cellophane-wrapped goodies she'd been working on in a lined basket. "There. Now, I can hand these out to remind the townsfolk of our duty to win the Seasonal Spirit Awards."

Vale shot me a sideways glance, and I stifled a smile. "I think it's Holiday Haven's year," my friend chirped.

"It better be," the bakery owner barked. "I don't want to win just the baking category. I want the whole thing. I can't wait to see Blanche Caulfield's face when I win it all."

"You mean, when the town wins," I corrected.

Wren realized her mistake and sniffed in dismissal. "Of course, that's what I meant." She picked up the basket. "Lock up when you leave. Be here all the earlier tomorrow."

TOWNSFOLK of all ages lined the street all the way down to the main square. Vale and I scarfed down some ho-ho-hot dogs and split a fa-la-la-lafel from a pop-up vendor at the edge of the market. After we satisfied our empty stomachs, we wound our way through the crowd to find the best view possible of where the sleigh would end up in front of the ginormous Christmas tree.

The chaos of excitement and noise put me on edge. "I don't know if it's a good idea for me to be in the thick of things."

My friend glanced up at me. "Why?"

A part of me wanted to tell her the truth about my messed-up magic. But I chose to keep the broken part of me a secret for now. "I don't like big crowds. They make me nervous."

"No problem. I've got just the place for us." Vale took me by the hand and pulled me off to the sidewalk. We slid behind people until she ducked into a doorway, dragging me behind her.

The darkened atmosphere in the room countered the bright and cheerful day outside. It took a second for my eyes to adjust. Tables and chairs were placed about the room. Dark wooden beams ran across the ceiling. Stools were stacked on top of each other in front of an elaborately carved wooden bar where a tall man that looked like he was in his late forties or early fifties stood, wiping down glasses. Orchestral music floated down from speakers in the ceiling, and I recognized the classic tune of *Good King Wenceslas*.

"Now, what would you two fine-looking lasses be doing in here instead of participating in all the festivities?" he asked in a British accent.

"Afternoon, Clarence. My friend here doesn't do so well with big crowds," Vale explained. "I was wondering if we could use the little balcony on your second floor to watch?"

It dawned on me that we must have entered the Whet Your Wassail pub, and that the man behind the bar must be the vampire proprietor. A little thrill ran through my body at my first meeting with one of his kind.

As if sensing my mix of fear and excitement, he grinned,

flashing his fangs at me. "I'm not one for big gatherings, either. If you don't mind me accompanying you, I would be happy to host you. It's upstairs and to your right."

Vale led the way, and we climbed out of a window to stand on a narrow metal balcony. From this height, I could see the whole layout of the town square with all of the people milling about in excited anticipation. Not being in the middle of things calmed my nerves, and I didn't fear any of my usual magical misfirings.

Clarence climbed out of the window to join us, bringing with him a tray. "I didn't know what your preferred libation might be, so I brought a little of everything. There's a cider I have imported from England, a yummy gin and tonic from my own secret stash, and a pint of my home-brewed ale."

After Vale took the cider, I chose the pint in order to taste the drink that the elves at Yuletide Yummies seemed to like so much. It took a simple sip to know just how good it was.

"That's amazing," I declared, lifting the glass in the air to toast its maker.

He grinned in appreciation. "I think so."

Vale nudged me with her elbow. "Tell him the name you came up with for it."

"You tell him," I muttered low to her, trying to ignore her insistent pokes.

My friend huffed. "But you came up with it. Tell him," she pleaded.

Clarence finished a sip of his gin and tonic. "Well, now I'm positively intrigued. What name would you bestow on my brew?"

With it being two against one, I gave in. "Fine, but you'll probably think it's silly. I called it Holid-ale."

The vampire threw his head back and chortled heartily.

"By Jove, that's not half bad. I think that's a fine name that the customers will enjoy."

"It's all yours," I offered.

A loud cheer from further up the street caught our attention, and we leaned out over the railing to see the source. At the very top of the main street, I spotted a large red object being escorted down the middle of the snowy road. Elves in red-and-green fitted tunics with a giant white *SS* displayed on the front flanked each side. A giant white and furry being followed close behind.

"Is that...an abominable snowman?" I asked in absolute awe.

Vale buzzed with eagerness beside me. "Santa's sleigh is coming down the street, and all you care about is one security detail Yeti?"

When I'd agreed to my one year of probation in the North Pole, I had no idea what spectacles and variety of supernatural lives I would be exposed to. And if there were this many wonders here to explore, then maybe the year would go by faster than I thought.

The noise of the throng rose to such an extreme decibel that I cringed even from my high vantage point. The closer the sleigh came, the more I could detect the details on it. Its wooden frame had a fresh coat of bright red paint. It had gold and green filigree intricate decorations accenting the sides. The black rails of the sleigh slid across the snow, leaving clean tracks behind it.

"I thought it required reindeer to move," I shouted at Vale.

She squealed and waved as the sleigh neared us. "They help guide it in the air and on the landings. But it's fueled by Christmas spirit, which is why it gets taken to all the different towns that make up the whole North Pole district right before the SSAs. It's when we're all at the top of our game."

As the revered vehicle got closer, a strange sensation fell over me. Maybe my resentment of my lack of holiday celebrations in the past didn't matter. Perhaps I could find the joy and happiness of the season right here and now. But that didn't make sense because I never liked Christmas. What was happening to me?

I shook my head, trying to clear away the fuzzy fog filling it. Clarence placed a cold hand on the back of my neck, and the world focused into clear view again.

"It's the effect of the sleigh. It'll pass in just a second," he explained.

"Thanks," I uttered, taking a few gulps of the ale to help steady myself.

The security elves parted the crowd in the town square to give way for the sleigh to reach its final destination in front of the huge tree. The yeti stood right beside the precious object while the elves created a perimeter to keep anyone from getting too close.

"There will be a few speeches made by the judges of the awards and then they'll let people get closer. Wanna go down and see it?" Vale asked, leaning over the edge of the railing to see as much as she could.

"I will need to stay here to man my bar as I hope several of the onlookers will stop in for dinner and drinks tonight," Clarence said, draining the last of his gin and tonic and finishing with a satisfied sigh.

"Rory?" my friend glanced up at me, the silent plea in her eyes hitting me right in the feels.

Against my better judgment, I agreed. We helped bring the empty glasses back downstairs and thanked Clarence for his generosity. For such a short girl, Vale proved her fierceness as she plowed through the chaos of onlookers to get us closer to the front. I feared experiencing the strange effects of the sleigh again, but I didn't want to disappoint the half elf after everything she'd done for me in such a short amount of time.

While we stood in a makeshift line to see the sleigh, I heard a familiar voice raised in anger near us. Nudging Vale, I pointed out Wren arguing with another woman.

"Why don't you go back to Garland Gale where you belong, Blanche," the bakery owner sneered, her face turning redder by the second. "We don't need your negativity here in Holiday Haven."

Vale grabbed my arm. "That's Blanche Caulfield. She's the head of Garland Gale's SSA committee. They won for the second time in a row last year. Ms. Wren *despises* her."

Blanche stayed calm despite the verbal attack. She picked up one of the wrapped bags from the basket our boss carried. "Oh, Wren. Do you really think you could bribe the judges with some of your less-than-stellar cookies?" She pulled the end of one of the ribbons and took a long sniff of the opened pack. "And...do I detect a scent of some unusual mixture of herbs? Perhaps something that isn't in the original recipe?"

Wren pursed her lips in annoyance. "What I put in my baked goods is my business," she insisted.

Vale and I let a few people in front of us so we could continue listening to the conversation.

"Not if it's something that might unduly influence the consumer of said goods," Blanche declared, retrieving a cookie and holding it between her perfectly manicured fingers. Instead of eating it, she crushed it in the palm of her hand and smelled the crumbs. "Just as I suspected. You've been shopping at Christmas Thyme for your special ingredients, haven't you?"

Our boss knocked the crumbs out of the other woman's hand. "I don't need you sticking your nose where it doesn't belong. The next time I see you, it'll be when you're giving up the overall award for best town to me." Wren turned on her heels and marched away.

"I saw her sprinkling something in the batter," I uttered to Vale as we moved with the line again. "But I didn't know what it might be."

My friend furrowed her brow. "Hmm, maybe I should tell Mama about that. I'm sure the coven wouldn't take too kindly to Ms. Wren adding anything she shouldn't into her baked goods."

The line moved fast enough to keep me from getting too overwhelmed with all the noise and bustling around us. As we got closer, I noticed the slight pulse of good energy and the unnatural shift to my feelings about the upcoming holiday.

"I don't know how long I can endure this," I said, gritting my teeth.

Vale wrapped her arm around my waist. "If you'll take a quick picture with me and the sleigh, then I promise to take you somewhere I'll bet you'll enjoy."

I raised one eyebrow at her. "Where?"

"Mm-mm," she denied me. "Not until you guarantee that you'll be in the pic."

I considered turning her down and making a quick run for it, but I just couldn't disappoint her. "Fine," I grunted.

"Yay!" she squealed. "I'm gonna get a selfie with my new best friend and Santa's sleigh!"

Her sheer joy was better than any magical spirit the sleigh could give off. "Don't you mean you're gonna get an *elfie*?" I joked.

"Now you're getting in the spirit of things," Vale complimented. "And that has definitely earned you a break!"

Chapter Four

Instead of walking down the length of the street with all of the people still milling about, Vale took us around the back of the stores, telling me what each one was as we passed by their back doors. She turned down an alleyway until we got to a nondescript metal door with no doorknob or handle.

"Now, the front of this building is Pine & Dandy's, which is a wood arts store. But the owner, Amos, went through some things a few years ago and hasn't been as regular about keeping the store open," she explained. "So, those of us who want to go here have learned to use the side entrance."

I didn't understand why my friend thought I'd enjoy shopping for things made out of wood, but I stayed quiet so as not to ruin her fun.

"There are two ways to get in. One is to figure out the secret password. Once spoken, the door will open. Let's try this one." She cleared her throat and spoke a little louder. "Hocus-pocus."

With anticipation, I waited for the door to unlatch or

swing open. Nothing happened. "I guess that one's expired. How do you figure out the correct password?"

My friend stood back and tapped her mouth while thinking. "It's usually something that gets passed along to regulars. I haven't been here in a long while, so I'm not sure what they changed it to."

"Then what's the other way to get in?" I asked.

Vale ran her hand over the metal until she found the right spot. "Reveal," she said in a low voice. The metal surface shimmered, and a keyhole presented itself. "See?"

It seemed like a trick straight out of the movies about young witches and wizards I'd snuck into when I was growing up. "That's cool. Then all we need is the key to get in."

My friend winced. "Yeah, the problem is since I wasn't planning on coming here, I didn't bring it with me. I guess we'll have to wait for another time."

I wiggled my fingers at her. "Ah, maybe not. Finally, something I'm actually good at."

Placing my hand over the keyhole, I concentrated the little magic I could control. I visualized in my head the ice growing from my palm and extending into the slot. Based on the little training I received from a not-so-reputable witch who figured out I could be useful to him, I waited for the ice to form into the correct notches, ridges, and teeth to fit the mechanism.

"There, I think that should do it." I lifted my hand away to reveal the head of my ice device.

Vale leaned closer. "Whoa. Did you just make a key out of ice? That's a nifty little trick."

Shrugging my shoulders, I figured she didn't need reminding of exactly what other more nefarious uses my particular magic could do. Or why I was here in Holiday Haven in the first place.

"Let's see if it works." Trying to play it cool, I ignored my beating heart as I gripped the created key. I blew out a breath to calm myself and placed pressure on it to turn.

The lock turned without resistance until it clicked once, and the door jarred open. A little thrill over my success buzzed through me.

"That's so cool," Vale exclaimed as she pushed her way inside. Remind me to call you if I ever forget my keys."

I took the key out of the hole and held it in my right hand. After we entered and shut the door behind us, low lights flickered on in the darkened hallway. We walked down the short corridor towards the brighter light and noise coming from a much larger room.

I didn't know what to expect, so when I entered the large space, I stood in awe as I looked around. Not one red or green decoration in sight. Nary a string of lights or the glitter of tinsel winked at me. The minimal warehouse-feel of the room felt both foreign and familiar at the same time.

"Okay, what is this place?" I asked my friend.

Vale smiled up at me. "Welcome to The Break Room. Holiday Haven's secret sanctuary for those who aren't feeling in such a jolly mood."

"Hey, I resemble that remark," Wyatt growled as he approached us from behind the bar. "I'm glad you took me up on my invitation to come see us, Vale. I figured you'd be out partying with all the rest." He turned his attention to me. "And I'm glad you brought your friend with you. Hey, Rory."

I narrowed my eyes at him. "I told you, only my friends call me that. And I don't have that many in the first place."

"Well then, welcome, *Aurora*," he corrected himself with a sly twinkle in his gaze. "That's a beautiful name anyway. It kind of fits."

I grimaced. "Do all the girls fall at your feet when you use corny lines like that?"

The hot guy grinned. "I never say what isn't true. And I

meant that your name fits with you living here in the area of the North Pole. Where we have the Aurora Borealis?" He pointed at the ceiling.

I looked up at the industrial-like ceiling with pipes running across it and metal lamps hanging down. "I don't get it."

"The Northern Lights," Vale explained. "You know, the cool colored lights that appear in the night sky?"

A little embarrassed, I shook my head. "I don't think I've ever seen them."

"Now, that's something we're going to have to rectify soon," Wyatt exclaimed. "You can't live here and not experience their wonder. Plus, all of the area is fueled by the energy of the auroras. They're a clean source of power."

My short friend punched the big guy in the arm. "You just like to burn it all up in your converted snowmobile."

Wyatt ruffled her hair. "What can I say? I like the wind ruffling through my hair at high speed." He tilted his head at me. "Any chance you'd like to go for a ride with me sometime?"

The word "Yes" wanted to leap out of my mouth, but I swallowed it down. "Maybe," I said, offering a sliver of hope. "I'll consider it if you ever earn the right to call me Rory."

He grabbed my hand and held it in his. "I like a challenge." His brow wrinkled. "What's in your palm?"

"Oh." I'd forgotten the key. "It's how we got in." With a flourish, I revealed the remnants of my magic.

He tried to take the key from me, but I snatched it away from him and switched it into my other hand. Risking a little fire magic into my palm, the instrument of ice melted into a small puddle and then evaporated into a puff of steam. With a smug smile, I waved the empty hand at him.

"Impressive." Wyatt nodded, his green eyes flashing with

admiration. "There was a time in my life where I would have found that talent very useful."

"But not now?" I pressed.

He held up both hands. "I'm on the straight and narrow now and have a good thing going here. I'm not doing anything to jeopardize it."

Something about his tone told me there was much more to his story. But since he didn't give me anything else to go by, I held back the slew of questions that flew into my head. However, I suspected that he and I had a lot more in common.

"Well, I'm glad you're both here to take a break," Wyatt said, directing us back to the bar. He stepped behind it while Vale and I perched on two wooden stools. "What can I get you to drink? And let me preface this by saying if you're looking for something sweet like cocoa, you'll want to go to the Candy Cane Cafe instead."

I wrinkled my nose. "I don't like cocoa or anything like that. I'm dying for some coffee, bitter and hot, but no one here makes any."

"Just coffee? I can handle that." Wyatt winked at me and yelled out, "Hey, Nutty, can you pour this lady a cup I brewed from my personal stash?"

My roommate scampered over the surface of the bar and stood on his hind legs. "Hey, hey, you sure you want some of *his* coffee?" His tail twitched, and he cocked his head to the side. "Pretty sure it's so strong that it'll keep you awake until New Year's. Although maybe that might stop you from snoring."

"I don't snore!" I admonished, my cheeks heating.

"Yeah, yeah, you do so. Heard you like a buzzing chain saw." The little squirrel did his best imitation until Wyatt and Vale laughed at the strange noises coming out of him.

"Just get me some of the coffee, please," I begged. As

soon as he bounded away, I defended myself. "I swear, I do *not* snore."

Wyatt shrugged as he wiped down the dark wooden surface in front of us. "Nothing to be embarrassed about. I definitely do. Loud enough to rattle the windows."

Nutty returned, pushing a tray holding a steaming cup down the bar with great care. "Here you go. Maybe you should let him add in some of his 'shine to give you an extra kick. Okay, bye-bye." He rushed away to talk to someone else before explaining what he meant.

I picked up the handle of the mug and breathed in the rich aroma of the coffee. "I seriously don't understand how anyone can function without this." Taking a tentative sip so as not to burn my tongue, I tasted it. The big guy and I had one more thing in common. "That's so good."

"Really?" Wyatt chuckled. "I didn't think there was anyone else in the world who would like their java strong like mine."

"Then you've been hanging out with all the wrong people," I declared, enjoying the bitterness of another sip. "I'll let you call me Rory all you want if you'll fix me a cup like this each and every day."

The man beamed with joy. "That is a deal I will definitely take you up on." He pulled something out from underneath the bar top on his side and set it on the surface. "Let me know if you want something a little...extra."

I stared at the clear liquid sloshing in the Mason jar. "What is it?"

"Moonshine," he bragged. "My grandpappy's recipe. I've got a still on my property where I make it just like he used to in the Great Smoky Mountains. It's a little piece of my former home that I brought with me."

"I thought I recognized a little South in you when you spoke," I said, smiling at him. "Tennessee or North Carolina?"

"You know the area?" he asked, his eyes widening with wonder. "My clan is from North Carolina. Sometimes, I really miss it there. Whereabouts are you from?"

My excitement over the good coffee must have gone straight to my head, and I had allowed the conversation to be drawn back to me and my past. "Oh, here and there. I'm not truly a Southerner. More of a wanderer. But I liked what I saw when I visited this one place. I forget what it's called, but it's got a famous road to nowhere that happened when a town got flooded."

"Ah, Bryson City," Wyatt filled in for me. "That's where we'd go to pick up supplies. Huh, fancy someone who knows my neck of the woods living all the way up here."

I felt the heat of someone staring at me, and I turned to face my friend. Vale had been watching our exchange in gleeful silence. "Don't mind me. Pretend I'm not even here."

"Aren't you going to order your own drink?" I asked, wanting her to stop making it weird.

"I'm not really into the harder stuff." Vale nodded at the Mason jar. "And I confess, I do kind of like the sweeter drinks."

"Nothing wrong with that," Wyatt exclaimed. "How about I get you a tall drink of water?"

"Excellent!" my friend exclaimed.

I put down my mug of coffee. "So, what kind of place is the Break Room?" I looked around at the few patrons scattered here and there.

"When I took over the space from Amos," Wyatt tipped his head at an older gentleman occupying a seat at the far end of the wooden bar, "it was just an old warehouse. But I eventually got him to let me fix the place up after he listened to all my dreams and planning long enough."

"Hmph, letting you have the space was the only way I could get you to stop badgering me," the older guy harrumphed. "Why don't you let the rest of us have a shot at the pretty girls? Why are you always first?"

Wyatt set Vale's glass of water down in front of her. "Because I'm far prettier and way nicer than you."

He dug around underneath the back of the bar and added a red-and-white striped straw with a snowman at the top. Lifting his fingers to his lips for her to keep his Christmasy secret, he added it to her drink.

The older gentleman slid off his perch and made his way down to where we were sitting and joined us. "There. That's me being sociable. Now you can get off my back about it at least until the new year. Call it your gift to me."

"What kind of gift?" Wyatt asked, acting all innocent.

"You know. Don't make me say it," grumbled Amos. He leaned in my direction. "Ya see, I don't take too kindly to this time of year on account of my Mabel passing."

My heart squeezed a little for the man. "I'm so sorry for your loss."

He gripped his drink a little harder. "She was a wonderful woman. My point of true north in my life. Without her...well, I've been kinda lost."

I didn't have any words of comfort to offer him since I'd never felt that way about anyone before. But I could sympathize with how he felt about the current season. "To be honest, I'm not a huge fan of this time of year either."

Amos stopped moping for a moment. "Then the Break Room is the right place for you. Only place in the whole North Pole district where you aren't bombarded with everything Christmas all the dang time."

Vale asked in a quiet voice, "You mean, you don't like Christmas?"

I glanced between her and Wyatt. I hadn't known either of them very long, but it wouldn't take too much observation of my life to figure out my aversion. And I was tired of trying to balance hiding why I was here with the difficulty of it all. "Honestly, it's always been kind of a sore point for me. Since I didn't grow up with any real family to speak of, I was usually on my own. When I was younger, I managed to get a coat and a toy donated to me, but the older I got, the less generous people would be with me. I usually found a warm place to hunker down until after the holidays."

I pretended I couldn't see Vale's lower lip tremble or the bar owner's pity in his deep green eyes. Finishing the rest of the bitter coffee in one big gulp, I allowed the burn of the liquid to distract me from their reactions.

"Then you must have done something pretty interesting to land you here of all places in the world," Amos stated. He looked me up and down. "What did they offer you? Less time to serve here than in the real world?"

My jaw dropped. "How did you know?"

"You aren't the first to be offered that sweet little deal. Heck, you live with one of the worst thieves the world ever created. Ain't that right, Nutty?" he called out loud enough for his voice to echo.

The squirrel leaped down from a table across the room and scampered across to us, scurrying up Amos's leg and onto the bar. "What's right?"

I smiled at my roommate. "Amos was just complimenting your skills that landed you here in Holiday Haven."

Nutty scratched his ear with his hind paw, almost tipping over. "Can't help it. I see a nut and I've gotta have it."

"Even though I happen to know you've had extra time added to your probation period?" I accused.

The squirrel shrugged his tiny shoulders. "I like it here. What's more time?"

Vale leaned forward so she could see him past me. "Or you could try *not* stealing and still live here once your time is up."

"Could," admitted Nutty. "But if people keep leaving their nuts out and I see them, what am I supposed to do?"

"Leave them alone or use your Kringle credits that they gave us on our arrival to purchase some," I insisted.

My roomie's tail darted back and forth. "Yeah, yeah, did that until I ran out. It's why I have to work my required job and others, like in here."

I raised my eyebrows and glanced at Wyatt. "You officially hired him?"

"What can I say?" the bar owner replied. "He works for peanuts."

"Literally," I joked.

Amos groaned. "Oh, no. Tell me you're not a fan of the puns, too."

Vale giggled. "Rory's actually come up with some good ones. Look, we took a picture with Santa's sleigh together, and she called it an *elfie*." The half elf passed her phone around.

"You know, for someone who doesn't take to the season all that much, you sure do look happy," the older guy accused.

I took my friend's spell phone from him and studied the picture. He wasn't wrong. "I think it had more to do with the company than anything else."

"Or maybe that heart beating in that chest of yours isn't as cold as you pretend it is," Amos countered with a quick wink. "Before you know it, you'll be deciding to stay here after your term's up, too."

Vale took her phone back from me. "I kinda hope so," she whispered low to me.

"You know what? It's getting a little too morose around here," the tipsy man declared. "Since it's a little my fault—"

"More like a lottle," Wyatt interrupted.

Amos ignored him. "Then I'm gonna buy everyone here a round. We could all use a little cheer."

Wyatt clapped his hands together. "What'll it be? Shots?"

I pointed at the Mason jar. "If that stuff is at all as potent as I suspect it to be, I'm guessing it would be a very, very bad idea."

"Sounds like a plan then," Amos cackled. "One for each of us."

I looked at Vale to see what she had to say. She bit her lip in hesitation. "Other than the cider at the pub, I don't really imbibe much."

"You don't have to if you don't want to," I insisted, not wanting to be a bad influence on her.

"Or if you're feeling adventurous," Wyatt added, "I could make you an apple pie shot with my moonshine."

My friend stopped worrying for a second. "So, it might taste sweet?"

"Just like a slice of apple pie," the handsome bartender promised.

"Aw, heck. Make us all one." Amos clapped me on the back. "Well, little lady, let this be your official welcome to the Humbugs."

MY HEAD THROBBED as if someone had a hammer and was slamming it directly onto my brain. Even opening my eyes felt like too much effort. I groaned and wiped the line of drool hanging off the edge of my cracked lips with the back of my hand. It took me a second to realize that some of my pain came from my tiny roommate pounding his feet up and down on my noggin.

His little upside-down head filled my limited vision as he leaned over my forehead to get my attention. "Get up, get up," he insisted.

"Why are you so chipper?" I rasped, trying to swallow but

failing since my mouth and throat were as dry as a desert. "And how did we both get home?"

The squirrel scrambled down my tangled hair and stood on my chest. "Doesn't matter. Right now, you gotta open your eyes and see. We've got problems."

I tried to follow his instructions but only managed to prop up one eyelid. "What's the big deal?"

With quick movements, he dragged the newspaper from the foot of my bed. The noise of the pages crinkling caused me to wince.

My roommate clambered up to my shoulder so he could read with me. I scanned this morning's *Hark! The Herald* paper, and even in my hungover haze, I couldn't miss the glaring headline:

Santa's Sleigh Stolen! Is Christmas In Jeopardy?

"Uh oh," I exclaimed, sitting up a little straighter. "Nutty...what exactly happened last night?"

Chapter Five

I winced against the sunlight beating down on my still-pounding head while dressed in a Christmas tree costume, standing near the actual town tree and holding the tray full of today's samples. Even though my entire body screamed at me to go home and wallow underneath the bed covers until I recovered, I had gathered all my strength and wits about me to make it to work. My squirrel roommate was right—we needed to act normal and go about business as usual to keep any suspicions of our involvement in the theft off of us.

However, working within close proximity to the crime scene did nothing to calm my nerves. The smart thing to do would be to keep my distance and ignore all the gossip and speculation. Actually, the smartest thing to do would be to hightail it out of Holiday Haven altogether. I had proposed that escape plan to Nutty, but my roommate convinced me that running away would make me look guiltier than staying. And although I still couldn't remember everything after imbibing the shots of whatever concoction that cantankerous Amos had encouraged us to drink, I remained certain that I had nothing to do with the disappearance of Santa's sleigh.

I approached another group of typical looky-loos, clambering for a look at the empty spot where the sleigh had been the day before. "Good morning, ladies. Would you like to try a sample of Yuletide Yummies' crinkle cookies? And there's some stollen bites here as well."

The lady closest to me turned with a little jump. "Oh, we're not here to buy anything. We just wanted to see if the news was true. The sleigh's really gone."

Her taller friend next to her scoffed. "Don't say it's gone as if it's a lost pet, Agnes. It's not like it sprouted legs and walked off on its own. Like the headline said, the sleigh was *stolen*. Who would do such a thing?"

"I don't know, Pearl. It's such a shame it happened in Holiday Haven of all places." Agnes clicked her tongue in disapproval. "Must be an outsider."

Pearl's eyes shot to mine, scrutinizing me from head to toe. "Or someone who's new," she grunted.

Their third companion pushed her way in between them, and I recognized the kind lady from the day before. "You two hens need to go peck somewhere else. It's not up to us to solve the mystery, and for all we know, the sleigh got misplaced by some rogue teenager who took it for a joyride. You're being ridiculous."

Agnes grabbed a handful of crinkle cookie samples and shoved them in her mouth. "But how would a youngster get past all the security? No, I definitely think some magical thievery is involved."

If I could conjure a hole to jump into right now, I would. Instead, I shuffled from foot to foot in utter discomfort.

"That's right," Pearl agreed, her mouth puckering with bitter contempt. "They should round up anyone who's ever been arrested and interrogate them. Or better yet, expel them from the North Pole altogether. Don't you agree, Cora?"

The friendlier woman shook her head. "Absolutely not. It's not our place to condemn first and ask questions later. Now, you two, shoo and leave this poor girl to do her job."

Agnes reached out to snatch a few more free bites, and I rotated the tray so she could only reach the fruitcake samples.

Pearl's mouth curled into a disapproving scowl. "I still think those who are not one of us should be watched." Turning her nose up at the tray, she gathered her shorter friend and stomped away.

Cora stayed with me and offered a compassionate smile. "I'm sorry, sweetie. You're new in town, which will make you a bit of a target." She patted my arm. "You'll need to toughen up that skin to survive things until they find the culprit."

"Thanks for the advice," I muttered, my shoulders drooping a little.

"Chin up, Aurora," she declared, surprising me that she had remembered my name. "Don't let them get under your skin. I'm sure everything will play out as it's meant to."

With a quick nod of her head, she left me standing by myself in the snow, wondering how long it would take for others in town to question my involvement based on my past. I trudged over to the bakery tent and slipped in through the back flap.

Vale finished with her current customers before addressing me. "What's wrong?"

"I don't think I should be out there today. How can I be within yards of the crime scene when I can't remember everything that happened last night?" I bemoaned, sitting down on the edge of the sled.

The half elf came over and placed a hand on my shoulder. "I don't think you have to worry. When I left you last night with the other three, you weren't doing anything more than perhaps disturbing the peace a little with your singing." She scrunched up her nose. "I don't think you should volunteer for the community choir anytime soon."

I ran a hand down my face. "Was I singing Christmas carols?"

"Absolutely not." Vale giggled. "That was against Amos's rules. You all had to sing anything *but* Christmas songs."

"But where were we going if we were outside in the streets?" I held my head and groaned, wanting more than anything to remember something of substance.

My friend patted my back. "You'll have to talk to the others to fill in the rest. Since I managed not to drink the shots, I scooted home. Now, I wish I had stayed so I could give you better reassurance. But one thing I'm sure about down to my bones—you had nothing to do with the disappearance of the sleigh."

I glanced up at her, guilt eating my insides raw. "You don't know everything about my past."

"But I know who you are right now. And my friend Rory isn't someone who would steal the sleigh." She nodded with more confidence. "Besides, even if you had, what would you have done with it? It's not exactly something that's easy to hide."

That little tidbit did cheer me up a tiny bit. "True. It's not like I could park it out back of our cabin and pass it off as a recent purchase."

"Right?" Vale glanced at the customers lingering at the table of the stall. "Listen, why don't you head back to the bakery and tell Ms. Wren that you need the rest of the day off?"

I didn't think going back home and stewing by myself would do me any good. "No. I think I can muster enough strength to make it, even in this ridiculous outfit."

My friend giggled. "Yeah, the new costumes Ms. Wren picked up on her trip to the North Pole city center didn't get any better."

I loaded the tray with more samples and headed back out to face the curious crowds. Even though I still needed the holes in my memory filled in, I no longer worried about my involvement in the sleigh's disappearance. And although I noticed more than a few glances and stares in my direction, I ignored the whispers and kept my head held high.

VALE INSISTED I accompany her home for dinner after the end of an exhausting workday. We walked past the last of the storefronts towards a large red structure looming ahead. On the right side of the building stood a Christmas tree lot with lights strung above it and wreaths hung on the small fence that encircled the area.

My friend waved at the short young man with pointy ears tying a tree to a customer's sled. "Hiya, Crispy." She leaned in closer to me and whispered, "Crispin's my cousin on my mom's side."

After ensuring that the tree was secure, Vale's cousin stood up straight, and I noticed the considerable height difference between the two family members. "Hey, Valey Girl," Crispin joked, straightening his knitted green-and-red cap on his head. "Who's the newbie?"

Vale tugged me closer to her and wrapped an arm around my waist. "This is Rory, my friend. So, you have to be nice to her."

The young man smiled in earnest. "Any friend of my cousin is okay with me." He shook my hand in his strong grip.

"I thought I saw trees being sold at St. Nick-Nacks," I observed.

Crispin nodded. "Mr. Cratchit gets his supply of real trees from me and then decorates them before they're delivered. But if people want to do things on their own, they come straight to the source."

I nodded in appreciation of his enthusiasm. "So, did you sell many trees today?"

Crispin perked up. "Business has been pretty brisk, but then again, around here, people decorate their trees all year round. Just sold a gorgeous six-footer balsam fir. That baby's gonna smell so good once they set it up."

I chuckled at his description. "Sounds like you love what you do."

"Oh, you have no idea." Vale's cousin practically danced as he waxed lyrically. "Being the one who gets to help others bring a little joy into their homes is a true privilege." He narrowed his eyes at me. "Speaking of, what kind do you have at your place?"

"Um...none?" I cringed a little when his mouth gaped at my answer.

Crispin perked up and crooked a finger at me. "Have no fear, I'm sure I've got exactly what you need. And since you're my cousin's friend, I'll give you the family discount."

I hesitated. "Well, you see, I've got this roommate, and it's really not fair for me to go and get a tree without him having a say," I rambled, hoping not to have to break the guy's heart.

Vale came to my rescue. "Crispy, leave Rory alone. She'll get one when she wants to. You coming to dinner with us?"

Her cousin shook his head. "Not tonight. Gotta finish up here and then I've got to cover a shift at the Merry Mart."

"Tell you what, I'll pack you some food to go. Wouldn't want you to go hungry." Vale poked Crispin in his stomach before giving him a hug.

Vale turned to face the red building of the Gingerbread

General Store. The white-framed windows featured tiny wreaths hung in the middle with candles flickering from inside. Greenery hung from the white porch railing with red bows tied around every pillar.

"Come on, let's go upstairs," my friend said, climbing the stairs and holding open the door for some exiting customers.

I followed Vale's lead and stomped on the doormat to remove as much snow as possible before stepping in all the way. Rows of stocked goods filled the expansive room on either side of the main thoroughfare. I expected most of the items to be food, but found clothing, tools, and other non-edible stuff displayed on the shelves.

"Papa? You here?" Vale called out.

A short man with a long white beard appeared at the end of the row. "There's my girl! How was your day?" He rushed over and gave her a big squeeze.

I smiled at their familial greeting, my heart squeezing a little at what I'd missed out on in my life.

"Everyone's been focused on the disappearance of Santa's sleigh," his daughter replied.

He nodded. "Here, too. It's all anyone can talk about." Her father rubbed his hands together. "Now, this must be the famous Rory Hart you've been telling us about."

My cheeks heated a little. "Oh no."

Vale's father put an arm around his daughter. "Don't worry, everything she's told us has been good. And I'm glad to see her smile more now and actually look forward to her job rather than dreading it."

"She does?" I asked, glancing at my embarrassed friend. "Well, at least she's spared the burden of wearing the costumes."

"What costumes?" he asked.

Vale grabbed my hand and dragged me away. "We'll tell you at dinner, Papa."

She navigated through the rows of goods and led me to a stairway at the back of the building. I tried to read all the labels and take in the different items as we passed.

"There's a lot of stuff here," I said.

My friend walked up the staircase. "Papa's motto is if you see it, get it. If we don't have it, we can get it. I meant to tell you that we're the ones who supply Wyatt with his coffee grounds."

I stopped moving right before we reached a red door. "No way."

Vale giggled. "I'll have him double his order next time. Or maybe I shouldn't so that you have to go to the Break Room and let Wyatt make you some." She opened the door wide. "Welcome to our home."

A fire roared in the nearby fireplace giving off a warm glow over the comfortable furniture set around the hearth. A tree, no doubt from Crispy's lot, stood in the corner with strings of popcorn and cranberries crisscrossing over the dark green surface. Multiple colored lights twinkled all over, sparkling off of the shiny ornaments hung from the branches.

A woman taller than me and wearing an apron exited the kitchen. "Aw, Vale, I was wondering when you would get here." She hugged her before giving me an embrace as well. "You are more than welcome in our home, Rory."

I stiffened in her embrace, unsure of what to do. "Thank you," I muttered, my hands still at my sides.

She let me go. "I assume my daughter has introduced you to my husband, Jingle. I'm Aster Sugarplum. I got a little behind with all the extra attention our town is getting right now, so I hope you're okay with some simple spaghetti and meatballs."

"Oh, I'll be happy with whatever you serve. Thank you for having me over," I gushed.

Vale's mother invited both of us into the kitchen to watch

as she finished prepping the meal. "I barely had time to throw the sauce in the slow cooker. I swear, nothing brings in more people than a scandal."

"The market was packed with people today wanting to look at the spot where it disappeared," added my friend. "Rory heard lots of different theories."

Aster stirred the sauce and started adding in the meatballs. "Ooh, like what?"

I kept the thinly veiled contempt of that Pearl woman to myself. "That someone sold it and stripped it for parts. That some kids must have gotten it and taken it for a joyride. But mostly, everyone wanted to know how in the world whoever did it got past the security team."

My friend's mother lifted her eyebrows. "I've been wondering that myself. Makes me think that some form of magic had to have been involved. Because that vehicle would have been warded beyond belief to keep it safe."

"Someone who has magic." Vale tapped her finger against her lips as if deep in thought. "Well, that only leaves...just about everyone in Holiday Haven."

"Not necessarily," her mother countered. "Whoever did it had to be able to wield pretty big magic."

That left me out of the running. At best, my broken magic might have only set the sleigh on fire or cast it in a block of ice. Relieved, I allowed myself to relax a little.

"I don't know about you two, but I've had enough talk about the sleigh. Vale, why don't you and Rory set the table? Your father will come up when he can, but he wouldn't want you to go hungry waiting for him," Aster instructed.

I stuffed my face with the delicious food, observing the banter between my friend and her parents. As a child, I had dreamed about what a family must be like, even spying through windows at some of my lowest points. To be included with Vale's family gave me a taste of something I'd longed for all my life.

I willed the tears welling in my eyes to stay put and focused on eating rather than the brokenhearted kid inside of me. I couldn't fix my past, but I could enjoy my present.

"I'm afraid I don't have anything to offer for dessert other than some leftover white chocolate and raspberry cheesecake," Aster said as she finished taking the dishes into the kitchen at the end of the meal.

"That's okay, Rory doesn't like a whole lot of sweets," Vale explained.

"Except your chocolate and raspberry truffles. Those are amazing, and I bet you have other combinations I'd like," I said, glad I could brag about my friend to her parents.

"Our Vale has always had a gift with candy making. I told her we could sell it here for her," Jingle said, stroking his long beard.

"Papa, I told you before, if I'm going to do it properly, I want to do it on my own." Vale sat back in her chair and crossed her arms. "I don't want to be seen as just your daughter anymore."

Her mother approached her daughter from behind and kissed the top of her head. "Your father and I just want to see you doing something you love. The whole world should have a chance to buy what *you* make."

A loud banging on the door interrupted the conversation, and Vale's father pushed his chair back and stood. "I wonder if there's a problem downstairs. I left Winkle in charge."

Loud voices echoed from the living room, and we all got up from the table to see the cause of the commotion. I followed Vale and her mother but stopped moving when Aster held up her hand in warning. Sneaking closer, I peeked around the edge of the room to spy on things.

"Mr. Sugarplum, I'm sure you're aware that harboring a fugitive is against the law," the elf in charge stated.

Vale's father stood as straight as possible, towering a full inch taller than the unpleasant outsider. "And I'd like to know who you're accusing of being a fugitive. Buzzy, surely you're not cooperating with this nonsense."

A tall, thin man wearing a dark green uniform took off his cap and scratched his bald head. "Well, I don't rightly know, to be honest. It's not like I get a lot of business down at the station. We've never had this kind of action in Holiday Haven before."

"Which is why I'm taking charge," the angry elf stated, stepping forward. He barked out, "Aurora Hart, you have been seen entering the premises. It will go better for you if you come quietly. Otherwise, we will assume everyone here is an accomplice and will also be charged."

"Wait now, Topper, nobody said anything about bringing formal charges. You said all you wanted to do was round up all those in town who are serving or have served probation in town to question them," the local lawman said.

"Deputy Buzz—" The authoritative elf took off his sunglasses, folded them, and put them in the front pocket of his crisp shirt. "I'm afraid you are not equipped to comprehend the serious nature of the crime that happened on your watch. Santa's sleigh is gone. And it didn't just poof out of existence. Someone must have done something with it, and as head of security, it's my duty to find out who as head of security."

I stepped out into view. "I'm here," I volunteered. "There's no need to do anything to the Sugarplums."

Topper grinned, high on his victory. "Please step forward, Ms. Hart."

"Mama, do something," Vale hissed, tugging on her mother's sleeve.

"Oh, I intend to. Nothing about how you have conducted yourself here nor what you are doing will be tolerated," Aster said in a firm tone that sent shivers down my spine.

With my head hung down in abject shame, I presented myself to the authorities. I held my wrists up for them to bind.

"If you're coming peacefully, then I see no reason to handcuff you, miss," Deputy Buzz said, offering me a weak smile.

"She's a known criminal," Topper countered. "I wouldn't trust her not to try something."

Vale's father stepped forward to intervene. "That's enough talk like that. Unless you have definitive proof of wrongdoings, I suggest you treat her with respect. Especially when you're standing in my home and store."

I turned to face my friend and her family. "I'm sorry for causing you any trouble."

Vale sniffed as tears rolled down her cheeks, and her mother placed a comforting hand on her shoulder. "Don't worry, Rory. I will make some calls, and we'll get this straightened out in a jiffy."

Without another word, I let the kinder of the two authority figures lead the way. My heart sank like an anchor in the ocean. I realized that no matter how many positive steps I took forward, my past would always drag me back down.

Chapter Six

"I'm sorry, we don't have any other places to put you all," Deputy Buzzy apologized as he unlocked the single jail cell. He gestured for me to enter.

Instead of a drab, dank hole of a room with minimal furnishings, I found Wyatt and Amos sitting in rocking chairs with their legs crossed, drinking something hot out of steaming mugs.

The older man snorted and smacked the bar owner on his arm. "Told you they'd drag her into this mess. You owe me a case of moonshine."

Wyatt got out of his chair. "Glad to see they didn't put you in handcuffs. Buzzy, how about a drink for the lady."

The confused deputy closed the door behind me and locked it. "Well, I don't know about that. The head elf of security is pretty unhappy already that we don't have a starker environment for you to stew in."

I turned to face him. "I don't get it. Why are we all here? Are we actually under arrest?"

Deputy Buzzy whipped off his hat again and held it under his arm while he ran his hand over his bare head. "Hard to say.

All I was told was that you were the first suspects in the theft of the sleigh."

Amos rocked harder in his chair. "Doesn't matter that they don't have a lick of evidence that any of us had anything to do with it. No, we're judged by our past alone."

"Yeah, yeah," Nutty agreed, hopping down from the window filled with bars. He scampered over and climbed to the top of Wyatt's chair, balancing on top of it. "We can't catch a break."

I stared back at the other three. "At least you've been here long enough for others to vouch for your character. I've been here less than a month. And I'm serving probation for charges of larceny."

"Ah, so that was your flavor of crime." Amos smiled. "Looks like we have a few things in common. If my Mabel were alive, you better believe my bitter behind wouldn't be sitting here now. Because I would have been nowhere near the rest of you last night."

I turned to face him. "What exactly did happen? I mean, they must have a reason as to why they think we did this."

"Well, we *did* go down to the town square to take a closer look at the sleigh," Wyatt said, grimacing.

"We did?" I didn't remember anything past falling off one of the stools at the Break Room.

Nutty jumped down into Wyatt's lap and stood on the big guy's knee. "Uh-huh, and we traded them some moonshine for a picture."

I smacked my face. "Of course, only we stupid few would create our own evidence against us."

"Not evidence." My roommate frowned. "All it proves is that we were by the sleigh. Doesn't mean we took it."

Wyatt pulled out his spell phone and pulled up the pictures. "Here. This is about as wild as we got."

I looked through a couple of the photos. It took me a

second to recognize the absolute joy on my face as I found myself surrounded by an odd ragtag group of reprobates posing with silly faces and fingers pointing in a *V* behind each other's heads. All except Vale, who stood in front with the biggest grin on her face in every single shot, especially when she was squished next to me.

I zoomed in on my face, a little jealous that I couldn't remember feeling the happiness the picture had captured. Of course, we could all have been influenced by whatever spirit the sleigh exuded, so maybe it wasn't authentic anyway.

"Nutty, I don't see you in all of these. Where did you end up?" I asked.

The squirrel's whiskers twitched. "Sitting in the driver's seat. Man, that baby's cushy." He twirled around and stuck out his little behind, shaking his booty and tail at me for all it was worth.

Amos snorted again. "Those nutshells they found didn't help our case when we tried to convince the head elf of security that we didn't do anything else."

"Wait a second. If any of this," I gestured at the small space we shared, "had something to do with last night, then why didn't they bring in Vale as well? She also partook of the shots that were poured. At *your* insistence, I might add," I said, pointing at my cantankerous cellmate.

Wyatt chuckled. "Oh, Vale didn't even finish the first shot." He took a sip from his mug. "Who do you think made sure you got home safely?"

I glared at my roommate. "I thought you said you did."

"Yeah, yeah, I did. I mean, I directed your friend as to which room was yours and everything." The squirrel scurried down the chair and sat on his haunches right in front of me. "You're not mad, are you?"

I took stock of my situation. Would things be any

different if I hadn't been drinking the night before? Probably not.

My shoulders slumped. "Not at you, Nutty." I leaned over and patted his little head. "I just think this is all pretty messed up."

"I quite agree," Topper interjected, standing on the other side of the bars. "If you're talking about how any of you could think that stealing the sleigh this close to Christmas would be a smart choice in life."

I backed away to put some space between us. "Not what I meant."

The ornery elf pointed into the cell. "I want you and you to come with me." He stood back to allow the deputy to unlock the door.

Amos pushed himself out of the rocking chair. "Come on, squirrel. Let's go see how *nuts* they think we really are."

My roommate followed behind the older gentleman, but before the group of them got too far away, Nutty turned around and scampered back in my direction. He pushed his way through the bars and clambered up my body until he perched on my shoulder.

"Whatever they do to you, make sure not to tell them about my secret stash inside the stove," he whispered into my ear.

I giggled. "Okay," I promised.

He kissed my cheek and scampered back down the hallway past the irritated security elf.

"So, that's why I haven't been able to cook anything," I said, touching the spot where Nutty had kissed me before sitting down in the chair Amos abandoned.

Wyatt raised an eyebrow at me. "One of Nutty's stashing places?"

I gawked at him. "How did you know?"

"Because he's got at least two going at the Break Room that I know of."

The handsome man rocked with me in companionable silence for a few moments. It gave me time to consider my predicament and whether or not I needed to make plans to flee the second I got out of here.

"If you're thinking of running away, I'd like you to consider something," Wyatt said in a quiet tone.

I closed my eyes, a little annoyed that I was so easy to read. "What's that?"

"Would you be running *towards* something or *away*?" he asked.

"Does it make a difference?"

Wyatt sighed and stopped rocking. "In my experience, not that I'm that much older than you, one way will hang over you and haunt every choice you make for the rest of your life. And the other is where possibility lies."

While he meant well, I couldn't help but be irritated with his wisdom. "Considering that you're in here with me, that must mean that your past isn't exactly clean. And if your family is from the Smoky Mountains in North Carolina and you're here, then doesn't that mean that you ran *away*, too?"

I sprinkled a little too much venom into my words, used to pushing people away rather than relying on them. Regret churned in my stomach, and I stopped rocking. "Sorry, that came out a little meaner than I meant it to be."

"Apology accepted," Wyatt said with ease. "And you're both right and wrong at the same time. I did a lot of stuff I'm not proud of. Most of it was dumb stuff when I was younger, but as I got older, I got into a motorcycle gang that committed much bigger crimes. Things went too far with the leader who was taking us all down a very nasty path in life. So, I worked with both the World Organization of Wardens and the International Magical Police to shut the whole operation down."

My eyes widened in surprise. "Whoa."

"Whoa, indeed," he said. "I was their inside man for quite some time, living a double life. And part of my deal was that my family got into the protection program. So, I literally can't go home because I have no home to go to."

I bit my lip to keep it from quivering. "I'm really sorry."

Wyatt sighed and leaned his head against the rocking chair. "Don't be. My choices put me in the position I was in. I just needed to make sure they didn't ruin my life or that of my family's. And as far as I know, they're doing okay."

"You mean, you don't hear from them at all?" I asked, hoping he wouldn't catch the slight tremble of emotion in my voice.

"I get a card every year and I send them one back. Everything's passed through a WOW agent that I became close to, and I probably shouldn't communicate at all to keep them safe." The chair squeaked as he moved it again. "But I'm a little too selfish to stop."

I started and stopped myself from asking more questions, but I was a bit selfish, too, wanting to know more about the man. "When was the last time you saw any of them?"

"Christmas more than eight years ago at my sentencing. The authorities had to book me right along with the rest of the gang members so they wouldn't figure out I was the one who helped bring them down. My grandpappy was the only one I allowed to come because I didn't think I could handle seeing anyone else," Wyatt said. "It wasn't long after I went in when they made it look like I died in prison and sent me here to serve out the remainder of my probation."

"But I thought you helped them," I countered without thinking.

He snorted. "I did. By all rights, I should still be in jail now for some of the things I participated in before I wised up. Once I got settled here, it took me a while to realize what a gift I'd been given at a second chance. And I wouldn't do anything to blow what I've found here."

I nodded but kept my head bent, biting the inside of my cheek to keep the threatening tears in my eyes from falling. "At least I don't have any family or anyone to miss me," I said, sniffling and rocking.

Wyatt stayed quiet, giving me space to tell my own story.

"I was in and out of foster homes as a kid. Got pretty close to being adopted when I was really little, but then the couple ended up getting a divorce and the father, who wanted me, figured I'd be better off in a stable home than with a single parent. So, back into the system I went." I tried to picture the man, but since I'd been so young, his face remained a friendly blur in my memories.

"Even though I moved around a lot, I always had decent grades when I went to school. Things only became a problem when my magic manifested. And then I spent all my time trying to hide my abnormality from everybody else." A particularly unkind echo of my past rose up in my mind. "Kinda hard to do when I would either set things on fire or cast it in ice depending on if I was upset or anxious. And I seemed to always be one or the other."

"So, that's what that key was? Fire and ice," Wyatt breathed out. "You know, you may think that makes you strange, but I think it makes you pretty cool."

"Well, the key trick is the only one I ever truly mastered, and that's because I fell in with the wrong sort. Someone who…let's just say whenever I failed, he created ways to force me to get it right." I still bore some of the scars left over from that unsavory period. "Still, that particular skill did help me survive for a long time. Although I did my best to take from those who wouldn't miss anything."

Wyatt chuckled, and the warm sound melted a little of my nerves. "You mean, you tried to act like a modern-day Robin Hood? Take from the rich to give to the poor?"

"If by poor you meant me, then yes." I smiled. "I really would try to take only what I needed to get by for the moment. Never anything of high value."

My cheeks burned from the shame of my past. I never told anyone the real truth to my life, but then again, I never stuck around anywhere long enough to allow anyone to get close enough to find out. And yet, in such a short time, I'd found a half elf, half witch who had somehow claimed me as her best friend, a roommate who kissed my cheek, and an impossibly cute guy who listened without judgment.

The sound of the other rocking chair scraping against the floor startled me, and I looked up. Wyatt scooted his seat closer until our knees touched. Taking my hand in his, he waited until I met his gaze.

"Like I said, you can either run away and be burdened by your past, or you can choose something to run towards. I chose a life here, and every blessed day, I work to run towards it." His thumb brushed my skin. "Whatever choices you make from here on out, try to go forward and not back."

"A touching sentiment, Mr. Berenger." Officer Noelle stood on the other side of the bars. "And one that I quite agree with."

I sighed and pushed myself out of the chair. "So, I guess my probation deal is off?"

"Not in the slightest. In fact, you're both free to leave at your leisure," she said.

I waited for her to unlock the door. When she didn't, I narrowed my eyes at her. "What's the catch?"

"What makes you think there's a catch?" she asked.

I pointed at the lock. "You're not letting us out."

"That's because I'm not the one who has the key." A sly grin spread on the officer's lips.

"Fine, if that's all it takes." Motivated to leave the cell, I didn't even require a whole lot of concentration or effort to create an ice key. Once it formed, I turned it, and the door swung open.

"Excellent!" Officer Noelle declared. "And you just proved my point."

"Which was?" I pushed.

She patted me on the back. "That you didn't steal the sleigh."

I looked between her and Wyatt. "I don't get it."

The laugh that tittered out of her was accompanied by the faint echo of jingle bells. "You had the ability to leave at any point you wanted to. But you didn't. I'd say that's more than proof of your good character."

I wanted to believe her. To grab onto this blind faith that she offered. But it felt like a trap. "So, because I was a good criminal who didn't make a run for it, that means I didn't steal the sleigh?"

"Well, that and a couple of other factors." The officer leaned against the bars. "Like Vale Sugarplum giving a sworn statement that she was with all of you, and that you left the area with the sleigh still in its spot. Her parents can also corroborate what time she escorted you home and put you to bed based on her phone call to them to let them know where she was."

The ball of fear in my stomach released, and I blew out a relieved sigh.

"Also, I'm pretty sure if you'd attempted any magic, you'd have more likely burned the thing to the ground than have made it disappear," she joked.

She had a point. "What about Amos and Nutty? Are they in trouble?"

Officer Noelle snorted. "Let's just say I had an enlightening talk with Topper. He's been sent back to the North Pole to report directly to his boss for his behavior. And I sent your friends on their merry way."

"Then who's going to carry out the investigation of the missing sleigh?" I asked.

Her eyes twinkled with a merry challenge. "If I have my way...you."

"What?" both Wyatt and I said at the same time.

I pointed a finger at myself. "But how can you have a criminal in charge of the investigation?"

"Because I can't be the one doing it. I'm not exactly an impartial party," the officer said.

An overwhelming scent of peppermint, evergreen, and mulled spices filled the cell. The officer winked at me before flourishing her fingers in the air. All at once, her entire appearance shimmered and changed from head to toe. The basic uniform covered by a simple puffy winter jacket melted against her body, changing from drab gray into bright red. The fabric billowed out into a long dress that fit her in all the right places. Sparkles danced across the surface like stars twinkling in the sky. A velvet cape tied itself about her neck, the ribbons careful to miss the silver hair that cascaded down from her left shoulder in one long braid.

"You can't be," Wyatt breathed out.

The lady chuckled. "Allow me to introduce myself properly. My name is Clara Noelle Claus, and on behalf of my husband, I am asking for your help."

Chapter Seven

My brain tried to argue with my eyes over what they'd just witnessed. Sure, I was living in Holiday Haven, a town in the North Pole district. And yes, I'd seen the sleigh that Santa supposedly used to deliver gifts to the whole wide world. But the actual physical manifestation of Mrs. Claus pushed me over the edge.

"I think I need to sit down," I moaned, allowing Wyatt to help me back into the rocking chair.

"Here. Drink this. It'll help." With another wave of her hand, Mrs. Claus produced a mug with a dark, hot liquid inside of it. She held it out for me to take.

I glanced up at her. "A part of me doesn't trust you, but since I already drank coffee you produced in the same manner before, I'll take it." My brain needed the jolt of caffeine from the dark roast.

She waited for me to take a few sips before she continued. "I'm sorry for the little deception from before."

"What deception?" Wyatt asked.

I pointed a finger at her. "She acted like she was my probation officer. Told me to call her Officer Noelle."

"No-o-o, not exactly," Santa's wife dragged out. "Technically, you asked what my name was. Noelle *is* one of them."

"Right, but not the most important name. Like your last one. Which is Claus. Meaning, you're married to *the* Santa Claus. St. Nick. Father Christmas. The guy who delivers all the gifts," I rambled, still a little mixed up with the whole situation.

Clara smirked. "And who do you think helps provide all the magic for the whole operation?" She wiggled her fingers at me.

"Wait, so you do all the work, but he gets all the credit?" Wyatt took a noticeable step away from her. "You must be pretty powerful to make it all happen."

She waved her hand in the air, and the ceiling above us changed from the roof to a view of the night sky with the Northern Lights dancing across. "This place has its own magic that helps fuel the whole operation. But I keep an eye on everything to make sure it runs smoothly. And losing the sleigh is a pretty big problem this close to Christmas." With a twist of her wrist, the sky disappeared, and the ceiling hung low over us again.

After forcing my gaping mouth closed, I gulped as the magnitude of her request hit me. "If you are who you say you are with all of your magic, then surely you don't need someone else to solve the case for you."

"On the contrary, I'm the last person who should be involved in figuring things out. For one thing, I'm at the tippity top of the covens of the North Pole district. If it's one of our own, then that puts me in an awkward position," Clara explained.

Wyatt grunted. "And then there's the little fact of you being married to the man who the sleigh belongs to."

"Exactly," she agreed.

"So, your brilliant plan is to ask for help from a witch with broken magic who just happens to be serving probation?" I pushed myself out of my chair. "I just don't see how that's going to work. Sorry about the sleigh and everything, but I'd rather keep my head down and stay out of things."

Mrs. Claus held up her hands in a plea. "Just hear me out. I think your position as an outsider is actually a benefit. Once word gets out that you all have been cleared, then everyone will start talking about what's going on. You might have the best vantage point to sift through all the town gossip and anything out of the norm."

"Think about it this way," Wyatt said, joining Mrs. Claus's side. "If you do figure out who did it, you'll be a hero."

"And if I don't, I'll still be everyone's number one suspect." I shook my head. "I don't think it's a good idea. I wish you all the luck in figuring things out, but I just want to stay out of things and finish out the rest of my probation." With a shrug, I exited the cell and brushed past her.

Clara's loud voice echoed after me. "If you figure out what happened to the sleigh, then I'll declare your probation over."

Of course, Mrs. Claus would make me an offer too good to refuse. I stopped in my tracks and turned on my heels to face her. "You could do that?"

"I'm the head witch in the entire North Pole. Of course I can. And I will if you can figure out what happened to the sleigh." She held out her hand. "Do we have a deal?"

I bit my thumbnail, torn between wanting to mind my own business and hope everything blew over and taking her up on the opportunity to get out of Holiday Haven as soon as possible.

"If I were you, I'd hurry up and agree," Wyatt prodded.

With one handshake, I accepted. The scent of cinnamon, oranges, and cloves surrounded us, and an energy sparked between our palms. Maybe Mrs. Claus didn't need a written contract to bind me to my word.

"Excellent," Clara exclaimed. "Then I'll leave you to it. If you find anything out, just let Vale's mother, Aster, know. She has a direct line to get information to me quickly. Oh, and you don't have to work alone." She winked at the big guy still standing next to me.

I snorted. "What makes you think you can trust him?"

"Because he could have broken out of here anytime he wanted to, too." She walked through the door of the jail cell and patted the bars. "Big animal like him would have no problem busting through candy cane. Good luck, Rory."

With another wink, she disappeared from view in a flurry of shimmery flakes that smelled like fresh snow. Wyatt and I both stared at the empty space she left behind before gazing at each other.

I narrowed my eyes at him. "What kind of a gang did you say you joined? And what did she mean by animal?"

The large man rubbed the back of his neck. "How about I get you out of here first. Then maybe you'll allow me to explain a few things and help you make a plan."

WHEN WYATT SUGGESTED GETTING OUT, I thought he meant leaving the small police station and hiding out in the Break Room. Instead, he surprised me by taking me to his place. I stood in front of a rather impressively large log cabin isolated in the woods. Just like the interior of his business, the exterior of his house held no trace of Christmas.

He fumbled with his keys, and I grew a little nervous. "Listen, I know we've spent more time together than most strangers do in the first twenty-four hours after they've met, but I don't think I'm ready to—"

"Relax," he interrupted me, gripping the key fob in his hand. "I'm not gonna ask you inside." With a press of a button, the garage door slid open. "I think you could use a real break from everything, and I have an idea of a way to let you lose yourself if only for a few moments. Wait right here, if you want."

He disappeared inside and left me alone with only my thoughts as company. The longer I stood by myself, getting colder by the moment, the more I started to freak out over the deal that I'd made...with Mrs. Freaking Claus! If I succeeded, I earned my life back. But my head came up with a thousand and one different ways I would fail. Glancing around me, I searched for the easiest escape route.

Something electric hummed to life inside the garage, and I jumped a little at the sudden noise. A bright light aimed in my direction as Wyatt drove a great big snowmobile, with two skis underneath the front, out of his garage and slowly approached me. He lifted the helmet off his head, and I longed to brush my fingers through his mussed hair.

"You wanna let the wind blow your troubles away for a little while?" he asked with the goofiest grin on his face.

"Not too fast," I said, clutching my arms about my waist. "Knowing my luck, I'd fall off the back and you'd be long gone before you ever noticed."

"Oh, I'd notice," Wyatt declared. He dismounted and handed me my own helmet. "But you better wear this just in case you do."

I scrunched my nose at him in fake anger and place the helmet over my head. It covered my entire face, and for a second I felt a little claustrophobic.

He placed his own helmet back on. "Can you hear me?" Wyatt's voice crackled through some speakers inside.

I jolted in surprise and giggled at my reaction. "Yeah. You're coming in loud and clear."

"Good. Now, I can tell you about the things we pass," he said, patting the seat behind him.

With a huge lack of grace, I managed to straddle the machine and settle in behind him. "What do I hold onto?"

"Here are the handgrips," he pointed out. "You'll want to pay attention to what I do. If I lean, you lean with me. Keep seated behind me at all times, and don't extend your arms or legs out. Wouldn't want them taken off by a branch."

"This sounds really dangerous," I complained, debating whether or not to trust the big guy.

He held his right hand over his heart. "I promise to take good care of you. And at any point and time you want to stop, you just let me know. But I have a feeling you'll be begging me to go faster long before you ask me to stop."

"We'll see," I said, making sure to grab the handgrips firmly. "You'd better go before I lose my nerve."

With a low chuckle that filled my helmet, Wyatt got back on the front of the snowmobile. "Okay, here we go."

The vehicle lurched forward, and I gripped my hands even tighter, squeezing my eyes shut. The wind rushed past me, and a little shriek of fear squeaked out of me.

"Open your eyes, Rory," Wyatt commanded.

"How do you know they're closed?" I responded, trying my best to find my bravery.

"Because if you were looking, you wouldn't be making a sound like a scared little mouse. Just trust me," he pleaded.

I allowed one eye to see, but as soon as I took in the view, both of them remained wide open. Fresh snow covered every inch of the land we flew over, but in my short time in Holiday Haven, I'd never noticed how beautiful everything really was.

We drove through untouched drifts, the tracks of the snowmobile's skis the only evidence of any life. Instead of telling me what everything was, Wyatt allowed me to enjoy the ride all on my own. He slalomed through a grove of pine trees until my laughter filled his ears. We climbed up a large hill until we reached a cliff that overlooked the entire town.

He cut the engine and hopped off. With strong hands, he helped me dismount, and then pulled off my helmet. The frigid air chilled my face, but the adrenaline coursing through my veins kept me from being too cold.

"You were right," I exclaimed, my breath coming out in puffs of steam.

Wyatt put a hand to his ear. "I'm sorry, I didn't quite catch that. Could you repeat it?"

I smacked his arm in play. "I said you're really annoying."

"Because I'm right." He wiggled his eyebrows at me. "I knew you would like the ride."

"I really did," I admitted to him and myself. "I guess I should have known a biker like you would have one of these."

Wyatt puffed out his chest. "Once a bad boy, always a bad boy." He looked up at the sky. "We'll head back before it gets fully dark. But first, there's one thing I really want to show you. Oh, and once you see it, don't run."

I wrinkled my nose. "Whatever it is you have to show me, I doubt anything will make me run at this point."

"We'll see," he said, placing his helmet on top of his seat and shrugging out of his jacket.

"Uh…Wyatt?" I asked as he pulled his sweater up and over his head. "I take it back. If you get nekkid, I can't be held responsible for my actions." I blocked my view with my hand.

"Just give me a moment," he requested. "I didn't bring a change of clothes with me, so I don't want to rip what I've got. Count down from ten and then uncover your eyes."

For some reason, I did as he asked, saying the numbers out loud and ignoring the familiar sound of a zipper and pants being pulled down. As I got closer to the number one, a strange energy electrified the air, and I dared to peek just a second early.

The man I'd been talking to threw his head back with his mouth wide open. With a grunt, he lurched forward, and massive amounts of black fur exploded out of his skin. Two enormous paws instead of hands hit the ground, and steam rose from the exterior of a very large and intimidating black bear standing where Wyatt used to be.

The animal chuffed and stomped on the ground a few times. It wiggled snow off its body with one big head-to-tail shake. When it turned in my direction, deep green eyes stared back at me.

"Wyatt?" I asked in a shrill voice.

The bear chuffed and grunted again. It lumbered toward me, and all of my instincts begged me to move my feet.

"Don't run, don't run, don't run," I kept repeating to myself through gritted teeth, squeezing my hands into fists in determination. "Even if there's a great big black bear that could eat me in one bite coming over, Wyatt said don't run."

The animal approached and stood right in front of me. It turned to its side, giving me a full view of its entire body. I reached out a tentative hand, wondering if I was breaking any etiquette by my great desire to touch him.

As if sensing my hesitation, the bear shuffled closer to me until its dense fur rested underneath my palm. Taking a deep breath, I gathered up all my bravery and allowed myself to pet the giant beast. I stroked the thick, coarse hair as if the bear in front of me were a tame dog. And yet, I could swear I heard a rumble reverberate in his chest.

"Silly boy," I said, gaining more confidence. "Bears don't purr."

The animal turned its head so he could look at me. I stared into its green eyes and found comfort in the depths of them. He moved his head until he nudged against my touch and rested under my fingers. With a soft chuckle, I gave his ginormous noggin a good scratch, earning grunts of satisfaction.

With deliberate care, the bear padded away from me, putting some distance between us. The same energy I'd felt before crackled through the air, and I covered my eyes to give him a little privacy. The growls of the animal morphed into the groans of a man.

After a few tense minutes, Wyatt spoke in a raspy tone. "It's okay. You can look again."

I peeked through my fingers and found him pulling his sweater back over his head. The fitness of his body had me drooling a little before he hid it under his clothes.

A little heat rushed through my body, and I tried to cover it up since he was watching me. "That was…"

"Scary?" he asked, picking up his jacket from the back of the snowmobile.

I shook my head. "New, but not scary. I should have guessed you were a shifter when you told me you helped take down that gang. Why else would wardens and the IMP get involved? Plus, I'm learning that Holiday Haven is really living up to its name. It's a sanctuary where anybody with an ounce of magic is welcome."

He broke into a wide grin. "Now you're getting it!"

Taking my hand, he dragged me out to the rocks at the edge of the overlook. He found a perfect spot where we could both sit down and look over the entire town. As the afternoon sun set, some of the lights from the houses and businesses twinkled back at us.

"Worth it?" Wyatt asked, bumping against me with his shoulder.

"Totally," I replied, nudging him back.

We sat in companionable silence, watching the colors change in the sky and more lights illuminate in the town center. The big Christmas tree with the star on top stood out in all its glory.

"I thought you could use a visit to my personal thinking spot," he said. "I used to come here to sulk when I was new to Holiday Haven. Thinking about the choices I'd made and how I missed my family. But little by little, I saw that I was the one isolating myself from all of them." He gestured at the town in front of us.

"How long did it take you?" I asked in an almost whisper.

Wyatt grunted. "Looking back on it, I think a little too long. I'm grateful for the friends I have now."

Looking out at Holiday Haven, I thought about my life up until this very moment. "I've been alone for so long," I admitted, sniffling a little.

He pulled a handkerchief out of his pocket and handed it to me like a true Southern gentleman. "I find that hard to believe since you've already got some loyal buddies in such a short time."

"Just one. Vale's really awesome. I think she's kind of adopted me," I said, wiping the tears from my face. "She has the kind of family I've always dreamed about."

"The Sugarplums are good people," Wyatt agreed. "But I wasn't talking about just her."

I frowned. "Who else?"

"Girl, I don't take shots of my moonshine with just anybody. And your roommate is pretty soft on you, too." He pushed a strand of my hair out of my face and tucked it behind my ear.

"What about Amos?" I asked, raising my eyebrow.

"Well," Wyatt drawled. "He's a tougher nut to crack, no matter how hard Nutty and me have tried."

I snorted. "So, a half elf, a bear shifter, a crazy squirrel, and a moody old man?"

"Welcome to the Humbugs!" he declared with a chuckle.

Thinking about each of them, a warm fuzzy feeling grew in my heart. "Oh my goodness, I've got friends. Plural."

"So, now you know you're not all alone in this new challenge you've taken on." Wyatt stuck his fist out for me to bump it. "Come on, don't leave me hanging."

I knocked my own fist against his. "Go Team Humbug."

We devolved into silly laughter and continued to watch the sun set on our town. Despite the chill in the air, the thrill of excitement and anticipation kept me warm. Or maybe it was the presence of a hot bear shifter sitting next to me.

Wyatt pointed at something above us. "Look up."

Tilting my head back, I gasped at what filled the sky. The first hint of the Northern Lights flickered like waves of color crashing above us.

Shivering, I gazed up in wonder at the awesomeness of their beauty. "I can't believe I live here."

Perhaps thinking I was cold, he placed an arm around my shoulder and pulled me closer against his warm body. "But you do," he said. "And ain't it grand?"

I leaned into him, reveling in his touch and in the moment. Wyatt had made me realize that if I ran away now, I'd be leaving a whole lot behind. Maybe that had been his plan all along, but I couldn't be mad at him for helping me see my potential for happiness. And for the first time in forever, I allowed myself to consider what I might have to run towards instead.

Chapter Eight

Wyatt had been right when he said I didn't need to figure out who stole the sleigh alone. I held a meeting at the Break Room with all of my friends and a few new ones to ask for their help.

"Let me get this straight." Amos slammed his drink down on the table. "You think you saw Santa's wife and that she asked you to find out what happened to his sleigh?"

"We didn't *think* we saw her. We talked to her and everything," I insisted.

Vale worked on opening a peanut shell from the bowlful sitting in front of my roommate. "Oh, Ms. Clara is definitely real and was there at the jailhouse. Mama called her as soon as that unpleasant security elf tried to arrest Rory."

I had yet to thank Vale and her family for their immediate support since I wanted to come up with something special and hadn't thought of anything yet.

"Putting aside whether or not you believe Mrs. Claus wants me to solve things," I said, addressing the rest of the people sitting around. "I've been pondering things, and I think Clara's right. Because of my status as an outsider, I might be able to observe more than those who are already a part of the community. And since many of you are kind of on the outside, too, I thought maybe you could help out."

A rock troll, appropriately named Rocky, spoke up, his voice grating like gravel. "Most everybody ignores me when I'm around, so it'll be easy for me to listen in on conversations. Count me in."

Vale popped one lone peanut in her mouth and passed the other two in the shell to my roommate. "You know you don't even have to ask. And my parents will pass on anything they overhear at the Gingerbread General."

Nutty stopped stuffing his face long enough to utter his usual, "Yeah, yeah, I'm in."

"Do you even need to ask?" Wyatt winked at me, and the eternal butterflies that kept flapping to life in my stomach ever since our snowmobile ride together flew back to life.

Amos leaned back in his chair. "Well, I typically would keep my nose out of things. But since our debauched night out that landed us in jail—"

"But not charged with anything," I quickly clarified.

"Right. Since that time," the old man continued, "I have decided that it's way more fun getting into trouble than staying home alone. And besides, it might be a hoot playing the role of a spy." He stood up and tipped his finger at the top of his head like he was wearing a hat. "Call me Pine. Amos Pine."

Wyatt snapped a towel at him. "You know, it might be helpful if you opened up your store on a more regular basis. That way, you can listen in on the customers."

Amos stuck his tongue out at his friend. "Only if you bring in more of your carvings."

His statement got my full attention. "What carvings?"

"You know those two big bears that stand outside the front of the store?" Amos pointed at Wyatt. "He carved those. My work is more refined, but everyone loves those log statues."

I had noticed them. Every time I walked past the wooden sculptures, I stopped to marvel at how much life had been captured in the subtle lines and strokes down the face of the wood. They had even given me a thought about what I might be able to do if I could just master my own magic.

The bar owner's cheeks got a little pink under his facial stubble. "I just took the whittling my grandpappy taught me how to do and turned it into a bigger hobby, 's'all."

"Well, that hobby of yours tends to bring in the customers and a pretty penny, which I give to you, minus my commission." Amos crossed his arms. "I'll open up if you bring me whatever you've been working on lately."

Wyatt thought about the offer for a moment. He slung the towel over his shoulder and extended his hand. "Deal."

The two men shook on it. I clapped my hands together, happy to have extra eyes and ears added to the cause, but the next problem was what to do with all the extra help. Where should we focus our efforts?

"Motive," Rocky grunted, interrupting my thoughts.

"What was that?" I asked, confused.

The rock troll cleared his throat. "Was just thinking we needed to narrow down who we were watching or listening to based on what we think the motive would be of the person— or persons—who messed with the sleigh."

Everybody stopped what they were doing and stared at him.

"Well, I'll be. That's the most words I've ever heard come out of your mouth. And they ain't half bad," Amos complimented.

Rocky shrugged his massive shoulders. "I like reading mystery books. It's what the hero detective always does. Figures out who has motive and then questions the suspects."

"Okay, this is good. So...why would someone want the sleigh? What's special about it?" I asked.

Vale raised her hand. "Santa uses it to deliver gifts."

I pointed at her. "Good. So, how does that translate into something someone wants to take?"

My friend bit her lips as she considered my question. "Um, maybe whoever took it wanted to deliver something themselves?"

Wyatt took a towel from behind the bar and wiped down the chalkboard with the list of drinks on it. Picking up a broken piece of chalk, he wrote down the word *Delivery* on it.

"The sleigh can fly, so maybe the culprit wanted to use it to fly themselves somewhere," Amos said. "Add that to the list."

"But doesn't the sleigh require the reindeer to navigate and land?" I asked, thinking about my short-lived time with Lumi at the reindeer sanctuary for the retired flyers.

"Hmm, didn't think about that. Cross my suggestion off the list," Amos demanded.

The chalk squealed as Wyatt drew a line through the word, and we all cringed.

I remembered the overwhelming feeling when I stood on the balcony at Clarence's pub. "I'll bet it's got some significant magic involved in it. Maybe someone wanted to have access to the power it contains."

Wyatt's eyebrow raised. "Now, that's an intriguing notion. And could somebody go check the door?"

"Why?" I asked.

"Someone's been knocking for the past minute or so." The bear of a man pointed a finger at his ear. "Shifter hearing."

"If they don't have a key or can't figure out their own way in, then maybe they don't belong here," Amos groused.

Vale slid off her chair. "You guys should consider changing

the whole speakeasy vibe. Maybe then this place would be full up of others. And who knows what you might hear then?" She padded out of sight towards the hallway that led to the door.

"If just anybody could come in, then wouldn't that change everything? I like that this is the one place where I can get a rest from all the holiday stuff," Rocky complained.

I patted his arm, forcing myself not to pull back at the odd texture of his thick skin. "If more people came in, it doesn't mean things would have to change. I just think others might appreciate a break as well."

"That's got to be his choice," Amos said, jutting his thumb at Wyatt. "But personally, I think it would ruin the whole Humbug vibe."

Vale came running back, waving a piece of stationary in her hand. "It was a couple of ladies from the Seasonal Spirit Awards committee. They've asked for everyone here to be sure to attend the final organizational meeting tonight."

"Why in the world would they want us there?" Amos asked.

Nutty hurdled himself over to Vale and snatched the card from her. His tail twitched as he read it. "Don't know. But all our names are on it. And a few others."

"Let me read it," Wyatt insisted. After a moment of perusing the names, he snorted. "This has the name of everyone in town who frequents this place. The plot thickens."

"Well, I'm not showing up just because my name appears on a list of those who don't care about Christmas," Amos declared, settling into the back of his chair as if he intended to never leave. "And I definitely don't care about those stupid awards."

"The awards," I muttered under my breath, remembering all the times Wren forced me to listen to how important it was for Holiday Haven to win. "Guys, I think I have an idea."

I made my way behind the bar and scooted in front of Wyatt, trying not to let my breath quicken as his body brushed against mine for a brief second. Retrieving the piece of chalk, I scribbled a word on the board in capital letters and underlined it.

"Spirit? What does that mean?" Vale asked.

I smiled at my friend. "Remember when we were on the balcony at the pub with the vampire?"

"Clarence let you watch the processional from his balcony? He's never let me up there," Amos pouted.

"Maybe if you were one of two good-looking girls, you might have had a chance," Wyatt teased.

Rocky shushed the both of them and asked me to continue.

"I felt an overwhelming sense of liking Christmas as the sleigh passed by us. Like I couldn't wait for it to come," I explained.

Vale scrunched her nose. "But isn't that how everybody feels most days?"

Wyatt and I answered her at the same time. "No."

I tapped the chalk against the board. "I think that's the sleigh's greatest value. The Christmas spirit it gives out. And that's why all of us have to attend the meeting tonight."

The others except Vale grumbled and complained. I waited for their protests to die down before continuing. "Listen, if whoever did this wanted to access the magic of Christmas spirit, then he or she will most likely be there."

"Oh, I get it," Vale squealed. "Maybe the culprit is someone who wanted to affect the Seasonal Spirit Awards."

"Whoever stole it might be trying to use the spirit that the sleigh gives out. We'll need to see if anyone gives out a particularly heavy vibe at the meeting," I instructed.

Amos tapped his empty glass at Wyatt while he moaned

loud and long. "If I'm gonna be forced to open my store *and* go to this silly meeting, then I'm gonna need some fuel."

"How about some of my coffee instead?" Wyatt offered. "We need you at your sharpest."

Excitement rushed through my veins. "Okay, then. Sounds like we've got a plan. Tonight, we'll go to the SSA meeting and then convene here afterwards to analyze our findings. Go, Team Humbug!"

The others murmured a weak response, but I ignored their lack of enthusiasm. For the first time in my life, I felt like I had a clear purpose. Like the puzzle pieces that never seemed to fit finally linked together. I didn't know what the picture of my life would end up looking like, but at least I had something to work with.

"How about a drink to celebrate?" Wyatt offered from right next to me.

An idea occurred to me, and I asked him to wait a second. Concentrating as hard as possible, I called on my magical energies. With my right hand, I created a small block of ice on the top of the bar. I held a picture in my mind of what I wanted. Using the fire power of my left hand combined with my ice magic, I melted and molded until I created a frozen stein complete with a handle and ready to chill a tasty beverage.

"Ha!" I exclaimed, dancing around in triumph. "I don't know why I was sure that would work, but it did!"

"Way to go, Rory!" Vale clapped her hands in glee. "Can you make me one, too?"

In less than ten minutes, every single Humbug had an ice glass of their own, including Amos. Wyatt poured the drinks and then held his high in the air. "Let's do this right this time. Go, Team Humbug!"

The others followed his lead and clinked their frozen mugs together. I floated on air, high on the success of my magic and my ability to coordinate the ragtag group of misfits. Placing my hand over my heart, I tried to keep it from beating out of my chest.

Wyatt put his arm around me and drew me close. "Just remember this feeling right here and now."

I snuggled into his solid side. "To cheer me up on a bad day?"

He leaned his head towards mine and whispered in my ear, "Nope. So that maybe, when you fulfill your deal with Mrs. Claus, you'll consider staying put."

Chills ran all over me, and all I could manage was a weak nod. Thinking about my future would only dampen my current buzz. For now, I needed to stay focused on the next step of attending the Spirit Awards committee meeting and narrowing down the suspects.

Chapter Nine

Who knew there would be so many people who took the Seasonal Spirit Awards seriously? I expected to find about thirty or so participants at the meeting. Instead, almost the entire town was in attendance, making my plan of the rest of the Humbugs infiltrating and observing a little less effective.

I encouraged my small team to spread out and see if they could spot anyone who was more enthusiastic than others. Vale and I stuck together while Nutty bounded off and disappeared into the crowd. Amos agreed to mingle but refused to be personable while doing so. His grimace and general demeanor caused many people to steer clear from him.

Wyatt chuffed at the frustrating man. "My grandpappy would say he's about as useful as a steering wheel on a mule."

Despite my frustration, I chortled a little. "At least he showed up sober."

"We hope," the big bear of a guy added.

"I'll position myself by the refreshments. Lots of people

will visit there, plus it's in the back where I'll fit," Rocky volunteered.

His large frame lumbered towards the multiple tables overflowing with all kinds of baked goods I recognized from Yuletide Yummies. Since Wren had given me a forced day off after my "unfortunate incident" of being taken to jail, I wasn't aware of her providing all the refreshments for the meeting.

Wyatt placed a warm hand at the small of my back. "I should go infiltrate as well."

Every part of me wanted him to stay by my side, but I forced myself to remain focused. Swallowing down my selfish desire down, I nodded. "Remember, we're looking for those who are supercharged with spirit."

"Yes, ma'am." He saluted me first before winking and walking away.

I took a little pleasure in watching his backside leave, and Vale caught my intense scrutiny. "Got a thing for bears, have you?" she teased.

My cheeks flamed to life, and I started to protest. But why deny what I clearly felt? "Yes. Yes, I do."

My shorter friend squealed, ignoring my urges for her to hush. "Ooh, I knew you two would make an interesting couple."

"We're not an anything right now. More like...friends with a possible option to upgrade," I mused, giving too much brain power to the thought. "Besides, I'm not even sure he likes me that way."

"Oh, he likes you," Vale assured me, hooking her arm around mine. "I'm just so happy for you."

I stopped her from jumping up and down. "You'll get us very unwanted attention if you keep doing that," I warned. "Now, try to contain yourself and go see what you can find."

She tapped the side of her nose a couple of times to

indicate our secret. "Got it. But don't think we won't be talking more about you and him later on."

I stuck my tongue out at her like I had the first day we met, and she returned the gesture before giggling and waving her fingers at me. Left alone, I wound my way through the crowd.

I thought due to my semi-arrest, most people would try to stay away. Instead, I got pulled into several conversations. I guess my short time behind candy cane bars made me more popular. It took a little finessing to avoid giving too many specifics, but I utilized my own trendiness to try and detect any extra Christmas spirit floating around the different groups.

Wren tapped the microphone at the front and cleared her throat. "If everyone would please take their seats, I'd like to get this meeting started." She surveyed the entire crowd with a sickeningly sweet smile that disappeared when she caught sight of the throng around me.

I made my way to a row in the back and sat between Wyatt and Vale, eager to hear about their findings. Unfortunately, Wren had a long agenda she wanted to get through, so the meeting droned on and on far longer than we anticipated.

"And I encourage everyone to make sure you vote in every single category and not just the one in which you entered. Of course, we're all under the honor system for not voting for ourselves nor just for our friends." Wren extended her arms out wide. "If all goes well, this will be the best Seasonal Spirit Awards we've ever had. And then we'll be in contention for the best town award."

Thunderous applause exploded throughout the crowd in front of us. Several people whooped and cheered while others stood up in solidarity.

Wren surveyed the audience with a wide grin. "Who's going to win the best town?"

"We are!" shouted most of the people.

I shielded my ears and leaned close enough to Wyatt so he could hear me. "So much for trying to narrow this down to a solid list of suspects. Everyone in here is full of Christmas spirit."

"I don't know," he said, looking at those sitting in front of us whipped into a frenzy. "This doesn't feel quite right. Then again, I've never participated before, so maybe it's pretty normal."

Everyone chanted, "Holiday Haven! Holiday Haven!" They stomped their feet on the floor until the whole place shook.

Wren held up her hands and waited for the din to die down to a quiet murmur. "I want to thank each and every one of you for helping us be the absolute best town in the North Pole. And when I bring that trophy home to dear old Holiday Haven, I hope you will remember all the sacrifice and work that it took." She brushed a finger under her eye as if wiping away a tear.

Vale tugged on my arm. "She's going to be a beast to work with during the whole SSAs."

"You're not kidding," I agreed.

"Please feel free to take any of the refreshments that are leftover home with you." Wren pointed at the back of the room. "And for those who received a special invitation to tonight's meeting, I ask that you remain in your seats, please. Thank you, one and all."

Vale, Wyatt, and I stayed put while others around us filed out into the main aisle. With a keen eye, I waited and watched to see who was left after almost everyone else filed out of the room. Nutty perched on Amos's shoulder and Rocky still maintained his position in the back by the decimated refreshments area. But a few others, including Clarence and a couple of gnomes with their long beards and pointy hats, remained.

Wren maintained her dazzling smile until the last of the stragglers left the room. Once we were left alone with her, she dropped the niceties and got down to business.

"Now, your names were added onto our special list because when we were inspecting the town, we noticed that none of you have added any decorations to the exteriors of your homes or places of business." My boss looked down her nose at each of us. "And I would like to find a way to rectify that problem."

"What we do at our own places is our business," Amos stated.

Wren sniffed once. "Except when it jeopardizes a major category of the Seasonal Spirit Awards. How can our fair town win if so many domiciles are barren of any sign of seasonal joy?"

Clarence looked around at the rest of us before standing up. "I, for one, do not understand why I am here. Whet Your Wassail always has greenery hung outside of it."

"Precisely, Mr. Griswold. You have done nothing more than your usual fare. And that just won't do." The owner of Yuletide Yummies approached him. "We need bows and twinkle lights. Red and green festooned over as much property as possible. A few evergreen swags and a wreath on the door are the bare minimum."

"It's far more than I'm willing to do," Amos protested.

"Yeah, yeah, me neither," my roommate added, shaking his fluffed-out tail at the unpleasant woman.

Wren clutched her hands into fists, and I leaned forward in absolute interest to see how she would handle direct opposition. As far as I'd observed at work, she did not do well with those who didn't say yes or jump at her every command.

"Mr. Pine, you barely even keep regular store hours," my boss complained. "While I was willing to overlook some of your transgressions in our small community due to the loss of your dear Mabel, it is high time that you took up the mantle that she carried with great aplomb for many years."

Amos stood up, and Nutty clung to the back of his jacket. "Don't speak of my Mabel like my loss is something that can be glossed over by hanging up tinsel."

"That isn't what I meant—"

"And as far as your Spirit Awards go," he continued, turning to face her. "I hope you remember that there are far more important things in this world than trophies." His bottom lip quivered a little, but he covered up the show of weakness by growling at the woman in charge and stomping out of the room without another word.

The rest of us squirmed in discomfort while Wren tried to regroup. "I apologize," she uttered.

"We're not the ones who need to hear those words from you," Wyatt said with his arms crossed over his chest.

My boss cleared her throat. "Well, all I am trying to do is encourage those of you with a clear lack of spirit to make an attempt this one time a year. I have heard the term Humbug used for those of you who turn your noses up at those of us with an abundance of Christmas spirit. Would you rather not be rid of such a moniker once and for all?"

"It should be the right of every individual to participate or not," Wyatt pushed as he stood up. "You've made your request, and now we get to decide whether or not to comply." He held out his hand to me.

I let him help me up out of the chair, and Vale joined me. The others took their cues from us and also rose to leave.

"Vale and Aurora, I expect much more from the two of you as my employees," Wren barked out in desperation.

I tugged on Wyatt to stop before addressing the thinly

veiled threat. "Ms. Wren, I will continue to do my job with the same enthusiasm I have provided since my first day."

"As will I," Vale said in solidarity.

"I do not question your participation, Miss Sugarplum. Your parents have raised you right in appreciating everything Holiday Haven has to offer. But I would be careful of where your loyalties lie," Wren cautioned. "It would be a shame if your family's reputation were to be tarnished by who you choose to hang out with. Or perhaps you could use your influence to encourage those you claim as friends to do the right thing. Just think about it."

I headed out hand-in-hand with Wyatt followed by the other stragglers at the end of the meeting. As we approached the back of the room, Rocky waited by the door and ducked through it right before us. We all drew in deep breaths of the frigid evening air to clear the confusion and irritation from our systems.

"Well, that was fairly unpleasant," Clarence declared as he approached us. "I felt quite like a little schoolboy being called to the front of the class for disobedience."

"And I like your understated decorations," I said to the vampire. "I don't think doing anything over the top is what's going to win or lose any prizes."

"Precisely," he agreed with a sigh. "Oh well, you are all welcome to come back to my pub for some cheer. And by that, I mean some of my Holid-Ale."

Wyatt raised his eyebrows. "Cool name."

"Your charming lady there thought of it." Clarence pointed at me.

One of the gnomes whose name I didn't know tugged on the vampire's arm. "We'll gladly take you up on your offer."

"Excellent. Allow me to lead the way, kind sirs." With a quick wave to the rest of us, the three of them trudged off in the snow towards the Wassail.

I'd hoped to have more information to work with after the meeting, but I felt as confused and stuck as I had when I'd agreed to figure out the mystery.

I scoffed. "I don't suppose anybody came right out and said they took Santa's sleigh?"

"No," Vale answered, echoing the other shaken heads in reply. "Mama was there longer than we were, so I'll be sure to ask her what she observed. But as far as finding anyone with an excessive amount of Christmas spirit, I think everyone in attendance qualifies."

Wyatt shifted his weight but kept ahold of my hand. "I've never seen so much enthusiasm for the awards before. Rocky, you've been mighty quiet all this time. What did you observe?"

"Hmm?" The rock troll shook his head as if waking up from a daydream. "I was just thinking about what I could hang from the outside of my cave. Maybe some lights hanging down like icicles would look appropriately festive."

I stared at the troll with an open mouth. "That's...not what I thought you'd say."

He shook his head a little. "I...I'm not sure why I did. At first, I tried to listen in on the small talk as everyone partook of the refreshments. But after a while, I stopped paying attention to the details and just listened to the organizer speak. She was pretty dynamic."

Wyatt let go of my hand. "Before you came here tonight, would you have given any thought to decorating your home?"

Rocky scratched a thick finger against his stony skull. "No," he rumbled. "I wasn't that interested...until tonight."

Vale snapped her fingers. "It's a spell," she said. "Someone in there cast some sort of charm over everyone. Maybe that's why they got all riled up."

"Yeah, but if it was a spell, why weren't the rest of us

affected?" I asked. "I mean, I have no compunction to put even a single ribbon outside of my house."

"I don't know," she replied with a frown. "I'll have to ask Mama what she thinks."

"I hope she has a good idea, because at this point, I'm feeling a little lost." I kicked my foot through a small snowdrift, sending flakes into the air.

Rocky rubbed the back of his thick neck. "I guess I wasn't that much help tonight. Sorry about that." He trudged away with thudding steps.

Vale glanced at Wyatt and me. "I think I'll head back to the Gingerbread General to see if Papa heard anything after the meeting and then talk to my mother. Goodnight!" She made no attempt to hide her wink at me, and I wanted the heat of embarrassment to melt me into the ground where I stood.

"I guess reconvening at the Break Room isn't going to happen. Not that there's much to debrief about." I kept my gaze down on the ground, afraid for Wyatt to see my internal frustrations so close to the surface.

Closing the distance between us, he slipped a gentle finger under my chin and lifted my head. "You didn't get the outcome you wanted. But that doesn't mean tonight was a bust. It just means there's more to figure out than you thought."

Overcome with joy at his words of comfort, I stood on my tiptoes and gave him a swift peck on his lips before my brain registered my actions. Realizing what I'd just done, I widened my eyes in shock. "Oh, I'm so sorry."

He wrapped his arms around me. "I'm not. But that definitely doesn't count as our first kiss."

"It doesn't?"

A low growl that sounded like the purr I'd heard from him when he stood in front of me in bear form emanated from his chest. "Not even close. But I don't think you're quite ready for that yet." He placed his lips on my forehead for a brief moment. "Come on. You and I are going to check on Amos, and then I'm going to take you to my happy place."

A thought popped into my head, and it took me the whole walk to our friend's house to fully recognize the sentiment. I looked forward to Wyatt opening up and showing me more about his life. But being with him was quickly becoming *my* happy place. And that both terrified and excited me all at the same time.

Chapter Ten

Wyatt lit the end of a piece of kindling until it glowed with an orange flame. He used it to light the pieces of wood stacked inside an old rusty barrel until a fire roared to life, casting light over his handiwork.

"This is where I go when *I* need a break," he declared, gesturing at the logs lined up around us.

It took me a second to recognize that each one had been carved with meticulous care. "I take it you have a thing for bears," I teased, brushing my hip against his.

"I've been known to think they're pretty great," he responded, placing his arm around my waist. "Do you like them?"

To be able to see each one in more detail, I risked a little of my magic to cast a floating light orb. I reached out to touch one of the bears standing on its hind legs but pulled my hand back at the last second. "May I?" I asked.

He nodded, enthralled with my interest.

My fingers traced over the lines and swells of the wood.

Although each of the bears was smaller in stature, I couldn't deny how much life existed in the timber.

"How are you carving these?" I asked, inspecting one that looked like it could walk off into the woods based on the forward movement of its captured position.

"Chainsaw to cut the logs down to the basic shape I want," Wyatt answered. "And then a chisel and some other tools to shave off the wood until the figure just leaps out at me."

I walked around another bear on all four of its paws with its neck stretched out and its mouth wide open. "He looks like he's trying to eat something."

Wyatt's eyes glinted with glee in the firelight. "He is. I just haven't figured out how to carve a fish jumping out of water yet."

I patted the bear's head in appreciation. "That would be really cool if you could. I hope Amos is giving you a good rate on commission."

The smile that had reached from the shifter's mouth to his eyes faded. "He does when he actually sells them. I was pleased that you had found a reason to push him to open his store once again. I just hope Wren's pet project and her words won't push him back into hiding again."

"He seemed to be pretty down when we left him," I admitted. "At least he was willing to let Nutty keep him company for the night."

Wyatt snorted. "The squirrel hasn't figured out that Amos stocks a lot of extra nuts from Gingerbread General just because he likes his company."

"Maybe they're good for each other." I thought about all my life spent trying hard not to make any friends. The loneliness of all my years weighed on my shoulders. "People shouldn't try to survive all alone."

The bear of a man strolled a little closer to me. "No, they

shouldn't. And I think those like us understand that statement better than most."

I allowed the light orb to extinguish and took a step in his direction. "It's so much better to have support from others who care."

"And it's easy to care for someone once she lets her guard down and allows people in," he challenged, stepping closer again until he towered over me.

I looked up into eyes that glowed with an inhuman radiance. It would be a perfect time to kiss, and yet fear held me back. Allowing myself a different kind of touch, I brushed my fingers through his locks, letting them entangle in the curls at the nape of his neck.

"Can I ask you something?" I murmured.

"Anything," he growled low.

I couldn't help the amused smile that spread on my face. "Is your bear separate from you? Or do you both exist together. In tandem."

Wyatt chuckled. "We're two different beings that share an existence. There, that's about as clear as mud for ya."

"No, I think I understand," I countered, still brushing my fingers through his hair and recognizing the difference from when I did the same with his bear's fur. "So, there are times when you disagree?"

"Mm-hmm," he admitted. "But right now, we both want the same exact thing." His eyes flashed bright.

Leaning his head closer to mine, he covered my lips with his. Instead of a passionate exchange, we both took our time with each other, tasting and testing. No rushing allowed. My body buzzed from the contact, and I wrapped both arms around his neck, pulling him closer.

Wyatt broke our contact with a little sigh. "I always knew I would eventually meet someone like you."

Still a little dizzy and disoriented from the kiss, I grinned with goofy glee. "So, what you're saying is that you're glad I was caught stealing?"

"In a way, I guess I am." He enveloped me in the warmest of embraces, swaying me back and forth as if we were dancing to music.

I snuggled into his massive chest. "You know, I used to hate my past. All of it. I'd wake up every morning loathing the life I'd lived. But now I wake up not focusing on what's happened before but thinking about what adventures I might have."

"Ah, you've finally learned the art of running towards something." Wyatt took a step back, placing his palms together before bowing. "My guru days are well and truly over."

I smacked his arm, certain he barely felt it. "Nobody likes the person who gloats. No *I told you so* dancing allowed."

"What about real dancing?" he asked, his voice turning a little shy. "There's this Yule Ball thing that's happening soon, and I've never attended before. But it would be my honor to escort you if you would have me."

His Southern manners and drawl grew more evident with his request, leaving me with no choice but to accept. "I'd be happy to. When is it?"

He blinked at me. "It's the Yule Ball, so it's held on the date of Yule. Which is four days before Christmas."

I squeaked in alarm. "But that's right around the corner. And according to Mrs. Claus, I have to solve the disappearance of the sleigh before then."

"Oh, right. The sleigh." Wyatt frowned. "It is frustrating that we didn't figure things out at the meeting."

"Or that we didn't consume whatever everybody else had that put them in some Christmas spirit haze," I joked.

At the same time, Wyatt and I thought about my last statement and stared at each other.

"Are you thinking what I'm thinking?" he asked.

"Depends," I said, holding up a finger. "First, tell me this. Did you eat anything from the refreshment table?"

He shook his head. "Nope. And I take it you didn't either."

"No, and neither did Vale. But Rocky was standing right there. Chances are pretty high that he couldn't resist eating something." I thought about the overwhelming amount of choices the tables provided.

"So, maybe someone laced the refreshments with a spell," Wyatt proposed.

A ball of stress clenched inside my stomach. "Not just anyone."

"You have a theory who it might be?" he asked.

I nodded, hating my idea but everything inside of me said that I was on the right path. "Yeah. Pretty sure it was my boss."

"Wren? Why would she risk doing something like that? She could get into a lot of trouble." The shifter threw another piece of wood into the barrel, and sparks of embers flew into the darkened sky.

"Only if she got caught. And based on what I've witnessed in my short time working for Yuletide Yummies, I'll bet she's willing to risk anything to win the Seasonal Spirit Awards." I gazed up at my companion. "You saw how she was tonight."

Wyatt mulled over my proposal from beside the fire. "It's not going to go over well if you accuse her without any clear evidence."

My confidence deflated a little. "That's a good point."

Hearing my despondency, he touched my arm. "I didn't mean to imply that you weren't right. Just that due to your precarious status as her employee..."

"Which I'm working for her due to my serving a probation sentence..." I added.

"Means you can't just come right out and say she did it. Not unless you get irrefutable evidence," Wyatt finished. "Which is going to take a little planning to figure out how to find it."

I snorted. "Maybe she's got a big garage by her house and the Christmas lights she has strung up spell out, 'Sleigh's in Here.'"

The bear shifter's laughter boomed and echoed into the night. "That would be convenient. But I doubt it would be that easy."

"I know," I sighed. "I guess I'll have to try to find some time to take a closer look when I'm at Yuletide Yummies."

"I'll bet Vale will help you."

I shook my head. "Under no circumstances do I want her to get involved until I'm more certain. It's one thing for me to make an accusation that proves false. What's the worst they could do to me? Other than kick me out of Holiday Haven and force me to serve a full prison sentence for my crimes. Which is definitely something to think about."

"And nothing I would allow to happen." Wyatt's brows furrowed. "If Wren Warbler is your number one suspect, then we might need to coordinate with the other Humbugs to investigate her."

"But I don't want anyone else to get into trouble," I insisted.

To stop my protests, he covered my mouth with his once again and kissed me silly until my knees turned to jelly and I forgot my own name. I kept my eyes closed even after he stopped his canoodling.

"Haven't you learned anything yet? Everything's better when you don't do it on your own," he insisted, wiggling his eyebrows for emphasis.

A crazy notion sparked in my head, and I pulled out of his arms. "You know, that's actually not a bad idea."

I strolled over to the bear carving with its neck stuck out and mouth open. Crouching down, I held out my hands. "If you want a sense of water, I know a better medium to use than wood."

My right hand glowed white blue as ice flowed out of it. Instead of waiting to add the heat of fire, I molded the frozen water with my left hand. Picturing what I wanted in my head, I willed the design into life.

"That's incredible," Wyatt breathed out while he stood right behind me, watching.

"Not done yet," I managed as I concentrated. "Now that I've got the bottom looking like a proper river, I want to capture the bear's meal just right."

Within a matter of minutes, the wooden bear held an ice fish in its mouth. Strange lights that mimicked the Aurora Borealis that ebbed and flowed over us glowed inside my own sculpture.

"It almost looks like it's wriggling," exclaimed Wyatt. "How did you do that?"

I wished I could put into words what being with him and finding my place in Holiday Haven had done for me in such a short time. But I couldn't find the right way to say it without sounding too silly.

"I don't know," I admitted. "Everything just seems to...fit."

He took both of my hands into his and brought them up to his lips. Giving them a chaste kiss, he pressed them onto his chest. "My sentiments exactly."

Under the Northern Lights, we explored how well we fit together until the chill of the air outweighed the heat of our passion.

With a groan, Wyatt ended our third explosive kiss. "I should walk you home."

"What a true gentleman," I teased.

"You wouldn't think that if you knew my true purpose was to elongate our time together and try to weasel out more information about you as we go," he said.

I took his warm hand in mine. "Well, communication goes both ways. Let's see all the things we can learn about each other during our walk."

By the time we made it back to my little cabin, I felt like I knew Wyatt even better. It surprised me to have thoughts of possible Christmas presents I could get him floating in my head. As we approached my house, I regretted that our time together was coming to an end.

A frown replaced his smile, and he pointed. "What in the world is that?"

Caught up in our little mini date, I'd completely missed the spectacle surrounding my cabin. Different colored lights outlined every single element of the house, blinking on and off in manic patterns. Someone had hung a wreath on the door with a hastily tied bow hanging askew. The sound of rapid hammering echoed in the air, and Wyatt and I rushed to find the culprit.

"Nutty, is that you up on the roof?" I called out.

The hammering stopped, and his tiny squirrel head peeked over the edge. "Gotta put up more decorations."

Wyatt flashed me a look of concern before pleading with our friend. "Hey, Buddy, why don't you come down from there and tell us what you've been up to."

Nutty's tail twitched with erratic frequency. "Amos kicked me out. Came home and there was a box of stuff sitting in front of our door."

I gestured my hand at the mess of decorations. "All of this was in the box?"

He nodded up and down several times. "Yeah, yeah. And a container of cookies."

I inspected the box and found the empty container with

only crumbs dotting the snow around it. "How many cookies did you eat?"

My roommate dug around the leftover decorations and pulled out a ball of tinsel, clutching it in his tiny paw. "Don't know. Lost count after eight." He thrust half the tinsel at me. "Here, you find a place to put this."

Accepting the metallic yarn from him, I watched as he scampered back to our house and up the sides until he stood on the roof. He sprinkled the spangly decoration over the top like they were seeds that would sprout more.

"If there were any cookies left, we could have had them analyzed," Wyatt said out of the corner of his mouth. "But I'm beginning to believe your theory about Wren."

"Forget my suspicions." I pointed at the squirrel zipping around the roof of the cabin. "We've got to get him some help."

It took me frantically raiding the oven to find some of Nutty's secret stash to set him up for capture. Once Wyatt had ahold of him, I called Vale's mother to find out what we needed to do.

Whoever had laced the cookies with whatever had made Nutty overdose on Christmas spirit had no idea the motivation he or she had ignited inside of me. If the culprit was indeed Wren, then she had just made a huge mistake.

Chapter Eleven

ster and Vale had come over as soon as we called to check on Nutty and his manic state. It took all of our efforts to get the squirrel to down a potion that Vale's mother had concocted to reduce the unwanted effects of the cookies. A good night in bed should get him back to normal by morning.

Pacing helped me to think, and right now, I couldn't sit still if I wanted to. "Thank you for coming over to help, Mrs. Sugarplum."

Aster finished pouring some of the leftover potion into a bottle. "I'm just glad it's something that could be handled quickly." She corked the vial. "If he wakes up in the middle of the night, another few drops of this should take care of things."

"Is there any way to trace whatever did this to Nutty?" I asked, pacing the floor outside my roommate's room.

Aster shook her head. "If we had more than a few crumbs left, perhaps."

"If there were any nuts involved in the cookies, there's not a snowball's chance there's anything left," I said, shaking my head.

Amos exited Nutty's room and closed the door with gentle care. "He's out like a light all curled up into a tight little ball in the middle of his pillow."

A little relief seeped through my stress, and I relaxed my shoulders a smidge. "Good. Poor little guy."

"What did I miss?" Amos asked.

I gestured at Vale's mother. "I was just bemoaning the sad fact that since Nutty ate all the cookies, we don't have anything left to test."

"Sure, you do," the old guy countered. "If you think there's something wrong with the cookies, I got a batch delivered with the same kind of box to my place."

"You did?" Wyatt asked.

"Yep. And I'll bet if you looked on your front porch, you'd find a similar package waiting for you." Amos plopped down on the arm of the couch, his wrinkled face stuck in a frown. "In fact, I'd lay a pretty big wager on all of the Humbugs receiving one."

Vale raised her hand to be heard. "Has anybody checked to see how Rocky's doing?"

Wyatt waved his spell phone in the air. "I called him to let him know about Nutty, but I didn't know to ask him about finding any box or anything when he got back to his cave."

Aster listened to all of us, shaking her head. "This is way more than any of us should be handling on our own. Maybe we should involve the law."

Amos snorted. "What? You think Buzzy would have the first clue what to do?"

"I don't really want to bother Clara with this since she has so much on her plate as it is." Vale's mother sighed in resignation. "But whoever did this has caused more harm than good."

"Oh, I'm pretty sure I know who did it," I fumed.

Vale bit her lip and glanced between her mother and me. "Rory thinks Ms. Wren is behind all this."

Aster's eyes widened. "That's a pretty serious accusation. Why do you think that?"

I relayed the story of catching my boss sprinkling something from a velvet bag into a batch of dough at Yuletide Yummies and then the encounter Vale and I witnessed while waiting in line to see the sleigh.

"Plus, the only motive for stealing the most powerful vehicle in the whole of the North Pole is for someone wanting to gain access to the incredibly powerful Christmas spirit it possesses." I paused in my tirade, waiting for my friend's mother to process my theory.

Amos grunted in agreement from his spot on the arm of the couch, listening to every detail.

"Wren Warbler can hardly be upheld as the only resident in town with a lot of holiday spirit," Aster countered. She paused, a quizzical expression spreading on her face. "Although, the ending of the awards meeting was a little odd. Come to think of it, I'm not sure why I got so caught up in all of the excitement."

Vale glanced up at her mother. "Did you happen to eat anything from the refreshments table?"

Aster gave the question some thought. "I didn't intend to as I was accosted by a few customers wanting to place some last-minute rush orders at the store. But then...yes, I did. I remember not being hungry, but when I was talking with Mrs. Berryman, we were right by the tables."

"What did you eat, Mrs. Sugarplum?" I pushed.

She glanced at me. "Some of the fruitcake. Which, now that I think about it is very strange since I don't even like fruitcake. And yet, I remember thinking it tasted absolutely divine. Oh my stars." Vale's mother covered her mouth.

"Exactly." I trudged a path back and forth as I connected all the dots. "If I'm right, then Wren has somehow figured out how to use the sleigh's magic to affect everyone else's sense of Christmas spirit. And while she might think it doesn't do any harm, we clearly know differently." I pointed at my roommate's bedroom door.

Aster furrowed her brow. "This is way beyond any of us." She took out her own phone and dialed a number. After the receiver of the call picked up, she spoke in a clear voice. "Code Rudolph's Nose, Clara...Yes, everyone is basically fine...okay, we'll be here." When she hung up, she turned to face all of us. "Better get ready."

"For what?" I asked.

A vortex of wind whirled in the middle of the room, and I rushed over to Wyatt's outstretched arms and huddled into his strong body. A blast of frigid air blew against us, and we struggled to stay upright. A light tinkling sound echoed in the middle of the indoor maelstrom, and snow whipped around. The scent of freshly cut fir trees and a wood-burning fire surrounded us. The swirl of snowflakes shimmered and solidified into a shape. Snow and light burst out of the center, and Clara Claus stood smack dab in the middle of my small cabin.

"Pardon my inability to knock when I enter this way, but as Aster has declared this an emergency, I felt that my presence was needed with expediency." Mrs. Claus dusted herself off and stomped her boots. She searched the faces in the room until she settled on mine. "So, have you figured out who took the sleigh?"

It took a few minutes until we caught her up to the present. Before she assessed the situation, Clara excused herself and left to check on Nutty. The rest of us remained quiet and in awe of the powerful presence of the head witch of the North Pole.

Mrs. Claus closed the door behind her as she left Nutty. "You did good, Aster, in stopping any further damage. I think the little guy will sleep off the effects and be right as reindeers in the morning."

"Oh, that is good tidings," exclaimed Vale's mother, placing a hand over her chest and heaving out a long breath of relief.

"But I'm afraid we have a more serious problem on our hands that needs to be addressed as soon as possible." Clara addressed the rest of the room. "It looks like the person who is using the sleigh to subvert the goodwill and spirit that it exudes is risking the very essence that powers the precious object."

Her words confused me. "In other words…"

"We need to get that sleigh back *now* or my husband will have no way to travel the world in time for Christmas," Mrs. Claus declared, placing her hands on her hips.

We all stood in tense silence, letting the gravity of the situation soak in.

Amos snorted. "Well, that sounds ominous."

"Indeed," agreed Clara. She turned to address me directly. "So, what are your plans?"

I pointed at myself. "Me?"

"Yes, you, Rory Hart." She nodded at me. "I think you've picked a suspect."

I wrung my hands together. "I have. Wren Warbler."

Instead of protesting my accusation, Mrs. Claus waited with patience for me to continue.

"I'm sure down to my very bones that Wren has something to do with the sleigh's disappearance. Why else would her baked goods cause such strong effects?" I asked.

Clara considered my logic. "Your theory about her motive is sound. But without proof, I'm afraid we can't move forward on it. Have you got any evidence?"

Amos raised his hand like a schoolboy waiting to be called on. When the venerable woman smiled at him, he cleared his throat. "I can bring over the cookies that were left with the box of decorations at my house."

"I could test them to confirm that they've been supercharged with Christmas spirit," Aster volunteered.

Mrs. Claus shook her head. "That won't be enough to implicate Wren herself. Anybody could have baked the cookies."

"What about me seeing her sprinkle extra ingredients into her batter?" I asked.

A frustrated growl rose in Wyatt's throat. "That would be your word against hers."

"If I weren't supposed to take another day off due to my 'unfortunate incident' of being detained at the town jail, I could bring in more baked goods to be tested," I said, annoyed for the first time at being denied the chance to work.

Trembling but still being brave, Vale stepped forward. "I could do that."

"I don't want you to risk your job," I exclaimed, looking to her mother to back me up.

"If my daughter wants to do her part to help you, then that is up to her," Aster replied, surprising all of us except Mrs. Claus.

"Anything you could bring back to your mother to test would provide more evidence to prove if there has been extra spirit added into the ingredients of the baked goods of the store," Clara yielded. "But it still wouldn't confirm that Ms. Warbler had anything to do with it."

"We're talking about a sleigh here, people," Amos said a little too loudly. Cringing, he lowered his voice a little so as not to disturb Nutty. "Shouldn't someone be able to search in garages or barns or anywhere one might stash a large vehicle?"

"The security team that you ran into already tried that," Mrs. Claus explained. "They tried to locate the tracking device on the sleigh."

"They couldn't find anything?" I asked.

Clara snorted. "Hence why some of you got the kind of treatment you did. Topper was more than frustrated because the tracking signal never activated in the first place. He figured one of you reformed or current probationary subjects did something to disable it."

"I hate to admit it," Wyatt said, rubbing the back of his neck, "but I would suspect us first, too."

"I wouldn't have the first clue how to disable anything. My only talent had been in unbolting locks." If I had been able to disable alarms, the chances of having gotten caught would have decreased significantly. "I don't think any one of us has the skills to bypass a tracker."

Amos made a clicking noise with his tongue. "That's not entirely true. Bypassing alarms used to be my specialty. But it's been an age and a half since I was in the business. Plus," he pointed at Mrs. Claus. "I'll bet all my teeth that any wards or alarms on the sleigh were mighty sophisticated so that only those who spellcast the protections could remove them."

Clara grinned at him. "Precisely, Mr. Pine. Which is why this whole thing has flummoxed me. Because while I understand why Wren Warbler would be at the top of your list, I just don't see how she could pull it off without being found out."

Unable to stay still any longer, I paced the floor trying to work through the problem. "Assuming Wren is using the sleigh in some manner to spike her baking, then we have to catch her in the actual act."

"I don't think it'll be easy to do that at Yuletide Yummies," Vale said. "Besides us getting really busy right now,

Wren will be devoting most of her attention to the Seasonal Spirit Awards and leaving the basic baking up to the others."

My pulse increased as a solution to our problem presented itself like a wrapped gift waiting under the tree. "That's it."

"That's what?" Amos asked.

"The SSAs." I waited for all of them to have the same revelation I did. When nobody else got excited, I gave a better explanation. "Wren will be completely wrapped up in the awards and wanting to make sure everything is perfect."

Clara circled her hand in front of her, trying to coax more information out of me. "Which means..."

"That she'll be doing everything she possibly can to make sure things go the way she wants them to." I glanced around at each person. "Guys, I think if we watch her close enough, we'll catch her using her baked goods to influence people in their voting."

Aster caught on and smiled at me. "That's some good thinking, Rory."

"But unless we tail her at all times, which is gonna be hard to pull off without looking really weird, how are we going to make sure we actually catch her in the process of using any Christmas spirit from the sleigh?" Wyatt asked.

I thought about Wren's encounter with her rival. "Vale, what was the name of the woman who argued with her before we took our picture together?"

"Blanche Caulfield," my friend explained.

"Ah, the SSA organizer from Garland Gale," Clara said. "Yes, I can imagine her and Wren not getting along well at all."

I paced the floor again, sure I was onto something. "There's one thing that trips up anyone who is up to no good every single time. Pressure. We need to rig the most important thing to Wren so that she makes a mistake."

"What's that?" Aster asked.

I glanced over at Vale, and we both smiled, exclaiming at the same time, "The baking category."

"She's entering her fruitcake," my half elf, half witch friend added.

Clara smirked. "That's a bold choice."

"If it's anything like the sample I had at the meeting, then there will definitely be a significant effect on the general voters and the awards judges," Aster said. "I wish we knew who they were going to be."

I glanced at Clara. "If only we knew someone who might be able to influence who was on the judging panel."

A wide grin spread on her face. "I think I see where you're going. If the stakes are high, then Wren might crack and do something that will prove without a shadow of a doubt how she's been using the sleigh to her advantage."

I pressed a finger to the side of my nose and winked at her.

"Leave it to me. If we want to raise the stakes, then consider it done." The scent of mulled cider and cinnamon floated in the air. "I'll leave the rest of you to work out the details."

With a flourish of her hand, the whirlwind of snow surrounded her, and Mrs. Claus disappeared from the interior of my small cabin, leaving behind a small flurry of snowflakes to melt on the wooden floor.

"That clears everything up," grumbled Amos. "Now what are we supposed to do?"

I caught Wyatt watching me, a slight grin on his lips. Returning the smile, I rubbed my hands together. "It's simple. Tonight, we get as much rest as possible. Because tomorrow, Team Humbug infiltrates the Seasonal Spirit Awards."

Chapter Twelve

I took a deep breath before entering the building hosting the SSAs. So much depended on what happened next, and my heart thumped hard enough in my chest I swore others around us could hear it.

"Everything's going to be fine," Wyatt whispered low in my ear.

Swallowing the slight lump in my throat, I nodded in half-hearted agreement. "I hope so."

He placed his hand at the small of my back. "Everyone is in place, ready to help. The plan you came up with is solid. Now it's time for you to trust in yourself and in us."

"Trust," I repeated. "I think I can do that." Taking a deep breath and letting it out, I rolled my shoulders back and kept my head held high.

Wyatt escorted me inside and through the throng of the different areas designated for each category of the awards. Despite my idea that it would be a simple affair, I had not been prepared for the massive size of the overall event.

"And I thought the enthusiasm at the last meeting was bad," I muttered as we navigated through the crowded area.

A fairy wearing a spiffy red outfit with a badge dangling from her neck hovered over to us. "Welcome to Holiday Haven's Seasonal Spirit Awards! Here's a ballot for both of you. Please mark clearly every entry you prefer in each category. When you're finished, you can hand it to one of our volunteers or place it in one of the designated boxes. Remember, your votes are important since the winners will move on to the overall regional awards. Thanks for your support!"

I accepted the hefty paper and glanced through the different categories. "Oh my word, there's so much more involved in this than I thought."

"The awards were meant to help build up the holiday spirit right before Christmas. It's unfortunate that the competitive nature of someone like Wren almost ruins it all," Wyatt said as he pointed in the direction we should head.

We walked by different displays in various categories. Vale had been right—if I'd researched the awards, I would have found something I could have participated in. I couldn't help but be amused at some of the categories of the first room we entered, including handmade holiday dioramas, original art in several different mediums featuring holiday themes, and some sculptures.

"I wonder where the food categories are," I mused out loud.

"Well, there was one thing I wanted to show you before we start our mission." Wyatt guided me over to a specific display. "I hope you won't get mad at me."

I stared at the placard in front of a familiar carving, reading the words out loud. "Holiday Wishes Come True by Wyatt Berenger and Aurora Hart."

"I added the holiday part so that it would fit the whole theme of the awards," he admitted.

The carved bear reached out to snatch the jumping fish

from the running river. Under the spotlights, I could see the absolute beauty of our talents combined. Unable to find words adequate to express the well of emotions bubbling up inside of me, I stayed quiet. But I slipped my hand into his and squeezed it, hoping he'd get everything I couldn't say.

A group of older women entered the room and chattered as they spread out to look at all of the entries. One of them sidled up close enough to bump into me. When I glanced at her, I found Cora smirking up at me.

"Glad to see you two together," she said, offering me a friendly wink. "And that you've managed to follow my advice."

I raised my chin a little higher in the air. "It was an excellent suggestion," I complimented.

She surveyed the bear and fish in front of us. "That's really amazing. I've already got a bear Mr. Hottie Pants made sitting on my front porch at home. Put a little Santa hat on top of him," she chuckled. "But if you're responsible for the ice part of it all, I'd like to talk to you about doing something custom for me."

My heart leaped into my throat, and it took me a second to regain some composure. "Uh, sure. I mean, I could definitely try."

"She made some cool glasses for me to use at the Break Room," Wyatt bragged. "They never melt and keep the drinks frosty the whole time."

"Your talents are completely wasted on that bakery. You should think about setting up your own business," Cora suggested, still staring at our work.

My jaw dropped. "I...I'm not sure they would allow someone like me to open a shop or anything."

"Oh, that's a load of reindeer poop," she declared with a snort. "If you could create ice sculptures that never melt, you'd have people knocking down your door. Me being the first in line."

Her confidence in me did strange things. Instead of wanting to hide my broken magic, I was proud to claim my powers. Letting go of Wyatt, I chose to give the kind woman a gift for her belief in me. Calling on both sides of my energies, I pictured what I wanted in my head and willed my magic to sculpt the object between both of my palms. Cradling it in my right hand, I lifted my left to reveal a blooming rose much like the one Clara had helped me create the first time I met her. Pink and red lights glowed from the inside of the ice.

I held out my gift to her. "Thanks."

"Okay, now you have to promise you'll let me book you first," she exclaimed, petting the petals of her flower. "Also, I think maybe the two of you should open your own place. You could call it The Bear & The Babe," Cora teased.

"We'll see," I answered her, placing a hand on my flaming cheek. "I hope you have fun with the awards."

She waved her ballot in the air. "You better believe I'm voting for you in this category. I'll get the rest of my cronies in on it, too. And make sure you check out my entry. I've decided to try and give that Wren Warbler a run for her money with my brown sugar pound cake."

"Will do," I promised over my shoulder as Wyatt and I left the room.

Once outside, he tugged on my arm and pulled me in for a crushing hug. I snuggled into his chest, processing everything that had just happened.

He rocked me back and forth. "I am so proud of you."

I backed away to be able to look up at him. "None of that would have happened if you hadn't entered your work."

"*Our* work," he corrected, gripping me a little closer and tighter.

I patted his back. "Can't...breathe," I joked.

He let me go, flashing me a sexy smug smile. "Sorry. Bear hugs are the only kind I give out."

With his surprise done, we focused on our very important mission. When we entered the large space with all of the food categories, we kept an eye out for our accomplices. We passed Rocky leaning against the wall on the perimeter.

I stopped in front of the large display featuring gingerbread houses of all sorts. It was hard to fathom the time it took to build up all the walls and roofs made out of gingerbread, let alone decorate with the frosting and other clever uses of candy.

"My Mabel used to love decorating gingerbread houses," Amos said as he sidled up to us. "She even won the category one year with her version of Holiday Haven's town square. I helped her figure out how to piece together the gingerbread to make the big tree."

I patted him on the back. "I'm sorry this is such a hard time of the year for you."

He sniffed. "Oh, anytime without her is hard. But she sure did love when everyone was geared up for Christmas. The SSAs were her absolute favorite thing to do. I'd grouse and groan about going with her, but in the end, we'd have fun discussing and voting for all of our favorites." The kind man wiped a finger under his eye.

Nutty popped his head out from his position on Amos's other shoulder. "Want me to argue with you over which of these entries is best? I'd have a better idea if you'd let me taste them."

"No!" Wyatt, Amos, and I exclaimed at once. Our reaction garnered us a little too much attention, and we walked over to a different display.

"What are you doing here anyway, Nutty?" I asked. "Shouldn't you be resting?"

His red tail fluffed out, and he cocked his tiny head at me. "Couldn't let you have all the fun. Wanna catch me a villain." My roommate's body stiffened, and his nose sniffed the air and his back leg thumped on Amos's shoulder. "Vote for that bread right there. It's got nuts in it."

"If you're gonna help, you have to stay focused," I reminded him.

He saluted me with his little paw. "I'm on it."

Wyatt tilted his head in the direction of the door across the room from us. "There she is," he murmured.

We turned to find Wren entering and greeting everyone as if she were the queen bee. "How's everything going? Do you have your ballots? Make sure you vote, especially in the baked goods category." While she talked nonstop, she failed to listen to anyone's actual responses.

It took considerable restraint not to walk right up and confront her about the cookies. But that would make me no better than Topper trying to arrest me with absolutely no evidence of wrongdoing. Instead, I nodded at my friends to make sure we spread out and began our vigilant observation of the woman.

Wyatt and I circled the room, accepting samples for the foods entered in taste categories. The closer we drew to the table where Wren stood, handing out bites of her fruitcake, the more I felt a compulsion of goodwill and joy.

"Whatever she's done to her fruitcake, it's overwhelming," I commented to my friend, holding onto his hand to keep me grounded.

He tipped his head closer to mine and whispered, "I feel it, too. That could become a problem if we're trying to stay focused."

Wren caught my eye and gushed at me. "Oh, Aurora, it's nice to see you participating in the awards. You as well, Mr.

Berenger. I'm glad you've both gotten caught up in the spirit of the season!"

I swallowed hard, trying to push back against the influence of whatever spell she cast. "It's been enlightening to see all of the entries," I admitted.

"Well, I hope you will consider voting for my submission." She flourished a silver platter with squares of her fruitcake laid out like they were crown jewels. "Even though you must have tried this for yourself while working for me, I think you'll find it particularly tasty today."

I forced my arm to stay by my side instead of reaching out to accept her invitation. "Actually, I don't like sweet things. I've never had any of your baked goods, as delicious as they look."

"That's...disappointing. And perhaps makes you a liability for working at my shop." Wren lifted her eyebrow at me with concern.

"Actually, I would think that would make me the ideal employee. One that you know would never eat your wares," I countered, taking a very important step away from her. Even that slight distance helped me fight off the intense feelings being forced on me.

I glanced at Wyatt, concerned with his ability to resist. His fingers reached out and hovered over the tray as if he couldn't help himself.

He frowned for a second, struggling to pull his hand away. "Did you use a traditional recipe?"

Wren flashed a wide grin at him. "I based it off the one passed down in my family over generations but have made it my own after years of perfecting it. Try some," she insisted.

A little bead of sweat broke on his brow. "So, what kinds of fruits did you put in it?"

"There are all kinds. Of course, raisins, both dark and

golden. And then some dried peaches and apricots, chopped cherries, some dried black figs—"

"Figs!" Wyatt shouted with a little too much enthusiasm. "I mean, I'm allergic to figs. Aw, I'm sorry, but I don't think I can try any of your fruitcake." Taking my hand, he tugged me behind him as he raced to exit the room.

As soon as we crossed the threshold, he let me go and bent over, grabbing his knees. "I wish we could use a feeling to implicate her."

I drew in some cleansing breaths. "If I didn't know better, I'd think the sleigh was right beside her. We're all at risk if we go anywhere near her."

"Perhaps I can help with that," a lady in a puffy jacket said from behind us, causing me to jump.

"Hey, Clara," I said, taking in her more pedestrian appearance. "Nice disguise."

She glanced down at her normal street wear. "I had to find a way to get to you without a whole lot of attention. And it looks like I'm here in the nick of time."

"Don't you mean, St. Nick of time?" I joked.

She snickered. "I'll have to remember to tell my husband that later. But for right now, eat these." She opened her hand and revealed two red-and-white-striped peppermints.

Wyatt popped one in his mouth before I could even remind her how I didn't like sweets. He sucked on the candy for a moment before letting out a long sigh. "Oh, that's better."

"What's in it?" I asked, eyeing the sweetie.

"Let's just say I used those cookies that Amos brought to Aster to help concoct my own temporary cure." Her bright eyes pleaded with me. "Just trust me. I've already handed some out to your cohorts."

With hesitant fingers, I accepted the peppermint and placed it on my tongue. The crisp sweetness at first turned my stomach a little. However, the longer I let it sit in my mouth, the more the effects of my talk with Wren faded.

"It's like the anti-spirit pill," I said, sucking on the candy with more relish. "So, can you just go in there and arrest her now?"

Clara winced. "It's still pretty dicey for me to be directly involved. Plus, this is still your operation. Do you think we have enough to accuse her yet?"

I agreed with Wyatt's sentiment when we first left the room. "No. A feeling isn't enough. But we could take some of her fruitcake and have it analyzed."

"And we will for sure," she promised. "But that won't do anything for the here and now. But I just spotted something I helped set up that might."

Wyatt and I risked walking back into the room. A camera crew surrounded Wren, and an elf wearing a white outfit lined with red piping with her hair pulled back in a professional-looking bun held a microphone.

A bright light switched on, and the elf spoke into the camera. "Hello, North Pole. This is Merry Mittens coming to you live, streaming over the Winternet, from the Holiday Haven Seasonal Spirit Awards."

"Did you set this up?" I whispered to Clara.

She nodded and held a finger up to her mouth. We both went back to watching the spectacle.

"I'm here with Wren Warbler, head organizer of this year's SSA committee for the town. Wren, tell me, how do you think Holiday Haven will stack up against all of the other North Pole communities? After all, Garland Gale has won the overall awards three years in a row. Do you think you have a chance this year?"

Wyatt snorted. "That's gotta hurt."

Wren kept a smile pasted on her face. "Of course, I wish all the luck of the season to our good friends in Garland.

However, I'm certain that Holiday Haven is ready for its turn in the spotlight this year. In fact, as head of the committee for our fair town, I've done everything I can to ensure we do our absolute best. I believe in each and every one of our entries and am proud how we have pulled together as a community to contribute to the holiday spirit this year."

"Ugh," I groaned, holding my stomach and glancing at Wyatt. "I told you I didn't like sickeningly sweet things."

Merry nodded at her interviewee. "And may I say that I am highly impressed with all of the entries that I've witnessed so far. But looking at the crowd gathered here surrounding the food categories, I can see that there is some fierce competition. As owner of Yuletide Yummies, I would imagine you would have a bit of an advantage if you entered anything into the competition yourself." She shoved the microphone back in Wren's face.

My boss kept up her appearances in front of the camera. "Well, I think all of us want the absolute best entries to be chosen to compete in the overall awards. And while I don't like to boast, I must say that my fruitcake is something that can't be ignored. Many are saying that my fruitcake makes them feel like they've eaten a little piece of Christmas." She picked up the silver tray and showed it off.

Clara giggled and nudged me with her elbow. "I already gave my friend there one of the peppermints."

The professionalism of the interviewing elf never slipped as the effects of whatever Wren had added to her baked goods overcame her. "I really shouldn't, as I'm supposed to stay impartial as I report from each awards event in all of the cities." Merry turned her focus to the camera. "Speaking of feeling like Christmas, what do you think happened to Santa's sleigh? And do you think its disappearance in Holiday Haven will have any effect on the outcome of the regional winner?"

Wren's smile lessened. "I don't think our town should be

penalized for the failure of the security team. And I believe that any and all justice for the sleigh's disappearance should be left to the authorities. Thank you." She offered a curt nod at the camera and walked away.

"Well, there you have it," the elf continued. "The Seasonal Spirit Awards are off to a good start. I will be reporting from each town's event as the day progresses. Be sure to continue tuning into your exclusive North Pole Winternet for the latest news. I'm Merry Mittens."

Clara, Wyatt, and I huddled in the corner. "I think we've effectively turned up the heat on Wren," Mrs. Claus declared.

I nodded at Amos, Nutty, and Rocky at the far end of the room. "And now, we have to watch and see how she reacts. With any luck, this pressure cooker of a situation will make sure her goose is well and truly cooked."

Chapter Thirteen

I should have known that Mrs. Claus's influences ran wide and deep. According to her, she'd set up others to keep cajoling Wren about Garland Gale's prior wins to stoke her competitive nature to a boiling point. With all of us on high alert, there was no way anything she did could escape our notice.

Wyatt and I circled the room with all of the food entries for the hundredth time when Wren strode in like a madwoman with purpose. Due to whatever she'd added to her fruitcake, people were gathering around her table more and more.

She pushed through the crowd, growing more incensed by the minute. "Get out of my way," my boss grumbled.

"We'll never see what she's going to do in this crowd of people," I hissed at Wyatt.

We only had one member of Team Humbug who could catch a glimpse from a completely different perspective. I rushed around the room until I found Amos with my roommate still riding on his shoulder.

"Nutty, we need you to try to see what Wren is doing by

her station right now." I pointed in the direction of the crowd.

The tufts of hair poking out of his pointy red ears perked up. "Yeah, yeah, no problem."

The squirrel scurried down Amos's leg and scampered here and there, avoiding being stomped on several times. With everyone else being attracted to Wren's table, no one noticed the path my roommate took. With great haste, he scuttled through the gingerbread display. However he managed it, he made it to the other side without damaging any of the entries. He scrambled up the layers of a gingerbread Christmas tree and hung off of it like a tiny version of King Kong, clinging to the decorated cookie star at the tippity top as he gazed over at whatever Wren was doing.

"It's not going to hold his weight," Wyatt worried.

I crossed both sets of fingers. "It's got to. He's our best chance at confirming our suspicions."

Rocky pointed. "The star is going to break off and he'll fall," he said in his raspy deep voice.

The noise in the area grew from a general murmur to a loud din of excitement. It almost became too deafening to bear. Wyatt winced more than once due to the sensitivity of his shifter hearing.

"The tree is starting to lean," he warned, pointing at Nutty's precarious predicament.

My roommate kept a tight hold while he strained to lean his body far enough out to get the best view over the back of Wren's table. Just as the gingerbread Christmas tree appeared to topple, the squirrel leaped off with his arms spread out, much like an action hero from the movies. He landed on the floor and somersaulted a couple of times before disappearing underneath the feet of all the onlookers.

"Do you see him?" I called out to my cohorts. "I hope he's not hurt."

Nutty's small figure reappeared as he scuttled out of the back of the crowd and darted over to us. He circled up my leg, and I held out my hand to provide him a perch. Out of breath, my roommate sat in my palm, his little chest heaving with his enormous efforts. He clutched half of the cookie star ornament from the gingerbread tree like a prize.

"What did you see?" I asked.

He glanced around at all of us waiting for his answer. "She sprinkled salt all over her baked goodies."

I wrinkled my brow. "That doesn't make sense. Are you sure she was sprinkling salt?"

"Yeah, yeah, you see, she took a small item out of her pocket, looked around, and tipped the item upside down. Then she shook it. Like this." Nutty mimed the actions of someone shaking salt over their food, using his whole body as he got more insistent and almost falling off of my hand.

"That clears up absolutely nothing," Amos groused. "Now what?"

"I don't know," I admitted, a hole of despair filling my stomach.

Nutty's tail twitched. "Don't be sad. Maybe you could use a dash of that funny-looking salt, too. It seemed to make those standing closest pretty happy."

My whole body went rigid on alert. "What did it look like?"

"Like tiny snowflakes falling in the middle of sunshine. Shiny and sparkly." He wiggled his paws in the air, mimicking snow. "And I might have to steal her shaker. It was real nice. All bright red with painted green-and-gold accents."

I gasped at the same time Amos and Wyatt glared at each other. Rocky sucked in a deep breath as he caught on. Nutty's little head whipped around as he glanced at each one of us.

"Did I say something wrong?" my tiny roommate asked.

"No. Something very, very right," I reassured him,

scratching him right between the ears. His back paw thumped on my palm as he leaned into my touch. "Rocky, see if you can go find our generous friend in the puffy jacket. Tell her we need her help."

Amos leaned in closer. "What's the plan, boss?"

"First, we need to see if Clara has any ideas about getting the crowd away from Wren. And then we have to figure out how to find that shaker that isn't a shaker on her person," I explained. "The only problem is, I can't figure out how."

Amos scoffed and waved his hand in front of his face. "Oh, that's easy."

"Why?" asked Wyatt.

"Because I was one of the best dippers in my time." Our cantankerous friend linked his fingers together and extended his arms out in front of him as if he were stretching to get ready. He shook out his hands and cracked his neck from side to side. "All I need is for someone to distract her, and I guarantee I can get that shaker from her without her feeling a thing."

"Are you sure that's a good idea?" Wyatt pressed.

"Listen, sonny, I may be old and rusty, but I've still got a few tricks up my sleeves. I didn't earn the nickname Famous Amos for my good looks." He jutted his thumb at his chest. "It was because I was known in a very wide circle as being able to pickpocket anything without getting caught."

"Until you got caught," I teased.

"Precisely." He winked at me. "Of course, I chose the option of probation here in this snow-covered land long before you were even a blip on this Earth. Met my Mabel and became a reformed man, living life on the straight and narrow. But I'm happy to come out of retirement if it means we can stop Wren from ruining Christmas."

Rocky returned, smiling at the woman he towered over.

He tipped his head in respect at Clara before leading her over to us.

"What's going on?" she asked.

I pointed at the fanatic crowd growing ever more manic as they got exposed to the sparkly sprinkles Wren had poured over her fruitcake. "We need to get all of them out of the room. Any ideas?"

She checked out the crowd. With a shake of her head, she sighed. "If I get everybody out of here, do you think you'll be able to accomplish what you need to?"

I looked for reassurance from Amos, who nodded his head. "Yes, I believe so," I answered.

"Okay. There's only one thing I can think of that might draw more attention." She unwrapped the scarf around her neck and handed it to me.

"What's that?" I asked.

A wide grin spread on her lips. "Me." Walking away from us and through the door into an adjacent room, we witnessed a flash of light and heard the commotion of rushing wind. A faint scent of ginger and citrus wafted around us.

A couple of squeals from someone in the other room captured the attention of those at the back of the crowd around Wren. Sooner than I expected, the rumor that *the* Mrs. Santa Claus was present at our town's SSA event spread like icing on gingerbread. Onlookers clambered to go gawk at her, leaving us alone in the room with Wren.

"Wyatt and Rocky, I need you two to cover the doors," I instructed. Both men grunted in agreement and strode away to take their places.

"Nutty, do you think you can help distract her?" I asked.

My roommate narrowed his beady little eyes with determination and rubbed his paws together. "Yeah, yeah, no problem." He bounded away, hopping to and fro until I couldn't see him.

Amos shook out his hands again. "Feels good to flex my skills. I feel more alive than I have in a long while."

I patted his shoulder. "Good luck."

Staying on the opposite side of the room, I watched the actions of my friends unfold. Wren stood by her fruitcake, confused as to what had just happened to her throng of affected people. She shrieked and began swatting at something on top of her head.

"Get off me!" she squealed, flailing about as she batted at the quick form of my roommate. "What in the world are you doing?"

Amos took his chance and walked in her direction. He jostled her a little as he acted like he lost his balance. "Oh, my goodness. I do apologize."

"You clumsy oaf!" Wren bellowed. "What is going on here? Where has everybody gone?"

I left my spot of observation and approached. "They've left to see a huge spectacle. Haven't you heard? Mrs. Claus has made an appearance at our very own spirit awards."

Wren stopped fussing with her hair and gathered her wits about her. Straightening up, she sniffed. "She's here? Then as the chairperson of Holiday Haven's committee, I should be the one to talk to her."

Amos stood behind my boss and flashed the item he'd sneaked off her. With relief and confidence, I stood in Wren's way. "I don't think so."

She drew up short and stared at me. "How dare you! Get out of my way! I must speak to Mrs. Claus," she demanded.

"Oh, I definitely think you'll be talking to her very soon. But first, would you like to explain why you've been lacing your baked goods with magic?" I accused, starting with a weaker allegation to see what she had to say for herself.

"I...I..." she stammered. Reaching up to brush a strand of hair Nutty had knocked out of her bun and push it behind her ear, Wren threatened me. "I don't know what you are talking about, Aurora. But you can be sure that come tomorrow, you will not have a job waiting for you at Yuletide Yummies."

"Ha!" Amos exclaimed. "That's rich."

"That's life and its consequences, Mr. Pine," Wren retorted.

"Speaking of consequences," I said, trying not to be too amused at her arrogance, "you don't need to fire me. Because I quit the second I came home to find my roommate sick because he ate all the cookies contained in a strange box with Christmas decorations someone left on our front doorstep. I don't suppose you would know who did that, would you, Ms. Warbler?"

She blinked at me, and a little color flamed to her cheeks. "I...don't know. And why should I believe anything a criminal says? You're probably lying. See, he looks perfectly fine to me." She pointed at Nutty who scrambled to stand in between my legs.

"Did you not think about the harm that could come from dosing the baked goods you allowed others to consume?" I asked, taking a step closer. "Or were you thinking that you could use Santa's sleigh to help yourself win your category? Maybe you even thought the magic contained in it could help you take home the bigger trophy. That you could win it all for Holiday Haven."

Wren's eyes darted around the room, looking for an escape from our inquisition. "I know for a fact that you were taken in for questioning in regard to the sleigh. Don't think you can deflect your crimes on me. I should call for the authorities," she threatened.

"Oh, they've already been alerted. And I'm not talking just Deputy Buzz. I'm sure Mrs. Claus has all the wardens of the North Pole at the ready," I warned. "If you want them to show you any leniency, then I would confess if I were you."

My now-former boss sneered at me. "Confessions are for criminals who've done something wrong."

Amos stepped forward and held his hand out in front of all of us. "You mean like someone who figured out a way to steal a very important object?"

He unfurled his fingers to reveal Wren's guilt. All of my suspicions were confirmed, and a giddy rush of excitement buzzed through me. There, in the middle of my friend's palm, sat a miniaturized version of Santa's sleigh.

Chapter Fourteen

Wren darted away from us, but Rocky blocked her exit. She turned and charged towards the other door only to find Wyatt waiting for her. Defeated, she gave up and stood with her head hanging down.

"I didn't mean any harm," she uttered low enough I had to strain to hear her.

"And yet, your actions have hurt others," I pointed out.

Nutty burst forth from beside my feet and occupied the space right in front of her. "Yeah, yeah, *me* being one of those you hurt." He hopped up and down, chittering at her in squirrel speak.

She narrowed her eyes at him. "But you're just an animal. How was I supposed to know that you would eat *all* of the cookies?"

A low growl rumbled in Wyatt's chest as he stepped forward, his eyes blazing bright. "What does his being an animal have to do with your actions? You shouldn't have put anything other than the regular ingredients into your baking."

Wren hung her head again, grumbling under her breath. I looked to the others to help me figure out what to do with her now that she was caught. But the expression on Amos's face caught my full attention.

"What's wrong with you?" I asked him.

He glanced back at me, his mouth forming a wide smile. "I don't know what you mean."

I pointed at him. "You're smiling."

"I am?" He lifted his free hand to feel his face. "Huh. I'm not exactly sure why, other than I don't feel as sad as I normally do."

"It's because he's holding the sleigh," Mrs. Claus explained in a loud voice as she strolled into the room past Rocky. "Hello, Wren."

The bakery owner's whole body trembled as she addressed the most powerful witch in the North Pole. "C-C-Clara," she stammered as she fumbled a half bow, half curtsy. "I didn't know you would be attending today."

"It was a last-second decision. But I came to provide back up for Rory here." Mrs. Claus circled around the guilty woman until she reached Amos. With an appreciative nod, she took the sleigh from him and cradled it in her own hands.

Wren's eyes darted to me, and my former boss fumed with rage. "What does *she* have to do with anything? She's just a common criminal."

"I'm not the one who stole Santa's sleigh," I reminded her.

She scowled at me but couldn't find a retort that wouldn't get her in hotter water.

With a nod of permission from Clara, I continued. "I wouldn't have even thought anything of it if I hadn't seen you sprinkling extra ingredients into your mixture at Yuletide Yummies. And then Vale and I heard you arguing with the woman from Garland Gale."

"Blanche Caulfield couldn't resist coming to our town just to rub my nose in her successes," Wren groused.

"But she was right when she accused you of adding

magical ingredients to your recipes unbeknownst to your customers, wasn't she?" I pressed.

Clara held up a finger. "Be careful how you answer. We've already taken samples from your store."

"And from the cookies you included in the box of decorations you left at my doorstep," Amos added, his scowl returning now that Mrs. Claus had taken possession of the special holiday object.

Wren took a step backwards as if putting some distance between her and us would protect her. "Lies. You have absolutely no proof that I did anything. And as far as me being seen putting anything into my doughs, that's hearsay at best."

Clara sighed. "Are you really going to try to make this harder on yourself? We have the word of Eve Hawthorne at Christmas Thyme plus all the receipts for the magical supplies you purchased from her. We have the testimony of your employees who say they have witnessed you adding extra ingredients into your mixer."

"Everyone's against me," the accused woman pouted. Actual tears welled in her eyes. "Why does no one want to see me succeed?"

"Why did you feel like you needed the sleigh in order to be successful?" I countered. "By everything I saw when I first came into Yuletide Yummies, you owned a thriving business. You would not have been chosen as head of the Seasonal Spirit Awards committee if others didn't see you as someone who could lead them to do the best they could. Growing up, I would have given *anything* to have even a fraction of the belief others had in you and what you had here."

Until the words came tumbling out of my mouth, I didn't realize just how upset I'd been at Wren's careless actions. She possessed so much and yet was willing to throw it all away just to win a simple contest.

Somehow, what I said broke through her flimsy defenses. Her shoulders slumped and she sniffled. "I know. It was a completely reckless idea. But I swear, I didn't plan on stealing the sleigh at all."

"Then how did it happen?" I pushed in a quieter tone, wanting her to keep talking.

"After Blanche accosted me right in front of everyone else in the town square, I just couldn't take the humiliation if we lost the awards this year. Especially to her." A large tear ran down her cheek, and she dashed it away with the back of her hand. "Yes, I've added in a few harmless herbs, spices, and other simple ingredients to my baking over the years. Nothing that would harm anyone. Maybe just give the consumer a boost in things like happiness or in their overall mood."

"And if they felt good after eating something from your store, then they'd be more likely to come back for more again and again, right?" Wyatt said.

Wren shrugged. "I honestly didn't see the harm in it. And then, as I stood humiliated right in front of the crowd who came to see the sleigh, the idea occurred to me that if I could just siphon off some of the powerful Christmas spirit the sleigh possessed, then I could harness it in my bakes."

"You've been acting with very little thought of the consequences to others for far too long." Clara crossed her arms over her chest. "Even if we didn't have a strong case against you about the sleigh, as head of all the covens in the North Pole, I couldn't let you get away with your actions. So, you might as well tell us everything."

"Yeah, yeah," Nutty exclaimed, scrambling up Mrs. Claus's red velvet clothes until he perched on top of her shoulder. "Start with how you got the sleigh so tiny."

Wren's eyes widened in fear. "I didn't mean to. Honest. It was never my intention to actually take it in the first place."

She held her hands up in front of her as if she could stop us from asking questions.

"So, why did you?" I pressed.

With a slight groan, she closed her eyes. "I just thought that the sleigh had so much Christmas spirit in it that it wouldn't hurt to drain a little from it. So, I snuck down to see it late at night."

"What about Topper and the rest of the security team?" Clara inquired.

Wren bit her lip. "Well, I didn't go empty-handed. I had whipped up a batch of ooey gooey cinnamon buns. I may have laced the icing with a little extra something that made the security team compliant and forgetful.

"I tried several different spells to break through the protective wards, but nothing seemed to work. And when the head elf of security seemed to be fighting the effects of my baking, I had to think fast."

Clara held up the sleigh in front of her. "I have to admit, we never thought we'd need to create any protection against a change in the size of the sleigh. You came up with a pretty ingenious way to scarper off with your prize."

"Yes, well, it was only supposed to be temporary until I could figure how to siphon off some of its spirit," Wren continued. "And then, one night after everyone was gone from the store, I accidentally knocked the sleigh over and noticed a little sprinkling of sparkles came out of it." Her eyes twinkled with excitement as she recounted her discovery. "And then I knew I had exactly what I needed to ensure my victory with this year's awards."

Her confession of her actions was more than enough to prove her guilt. And yet, the whole thing still felt incomplete.

"You knew about all of us being taken into the jail, didn't you?" I accused.

Her eyes dropped to the floor. "Yes. I figured there wasn't

any harm in letting the authorities assume those with criminal backgrounds were behind it all. If they figured out you were innocent, then they'd let you go. Although I admit, I expected them to keep you far longer than they did."

"You can thank me for that," Clara said. She snapped her fingers, and two enormous Yetis in full uniform entered the room followed by Deputy Buzz.

The older man took his hat off and scratched the top of his bald pate. "I'll never understand why people judge others by their past and not by how they live their lives now. While these fine folks have served their time for what they did in the past," he gestured around the room at the rest of the Humbugs, "they have acted with kindness and honor, which makes them A-okay in my estimate."

"Well said, Buzzy," Mrs. Claus agreed. "And now, I'd like you to make sure they transfer Mrs. Warbler to a jail cell where the bars are made from tougher stuff than candy canes."

The Yetis stepped forward and flanked Wren. Despite all her blustering from before, she no longer fought against the fate she had created for herself with her heinous actions.

They almost had her out of the room before a thought occurred to me. "Wait!" I cried out. "There's still one thing we haven't solved."

Wren glanced over her shoulder. "What's that?"

I closed the distance between us. "After you took what you needed, why didn't you return the sleigh to normal?" I demanded.

She shrugged with indifference. "I tried, but nothing I did worked."

Clara glared at her. "So, you figured if you couldn't return it the way that it was, you might as well use all the Christmas spirit you could get out of it, right?"

It took an angry reprimand from Santa's wife to finally

reach Wren. She hung her head. "I'm really sorry," she uttered in a weak voice as the guards and Deputy Buzz escorted her out the door.

I stood in absolute silence with the others, the adrenaline of catching the culprit still burning in my veins.

Amos broke the quiet first with a derisive snort. "The only thing that woman is sorry for is getting caught."

Rocky and Wyatt grumbled in agreement, but I kept my eyes on Clara. No matter how hard I tried, I couldn't read the expression on her face as she stared at the small object still cradled in her palm.

"Since you're the most powerful witch here, I assume you can counteract whatever spell Wren cast and return the sleigh to its normal size, right?" I proposed.

She shook her head. "I doubt it. That woman has no idea what she did in draining all of the spirit inside of it. At this point, the sleigh as it is would be more useful as an ornament to hang on a tree."

"What are you saying?" Wyatt asked.

Mrs. Claus looked up and faced all of us. "I'm saying that I'm pretty sure that the sleigh is broken beyond repair." She held the object out in front of her. "And if somebody doesn't come up with a miracle, I don't have any idea how my husband is going to be able to deliver presents this Christmas."

Chapter Fifteen

Having Santa's wife declare that Christmas might be canceled tore me up inside. No, I had not experienced a lot of happiness surrounding the holiday, but millions of others did. But I couldn't solve the sleigh's disappearance only to find out that it didn't make a difference to the holidays.

"There must be something we can do," I insisted. "Can't you have a new sleigh made in time?"

Clara sighed. "The sleigh wasn't just something my husband rode in. There was a lot of magic used during its creation. It took a lot of time and effort to craft it into the perfect vehicle. More than just the few days we have now."

"Well, there must be *something* we can do." I looked around at my other cohorts. "Amos, you do woodwork."

The older man held up his hands. "Hey, my work is on a much smaller scale. If you wanted a custom wooden dashboard, I could maybe knock that out in a few months. But this is way beyond me."

Wyatt stood across from me, offering me an apologetic wince when my attention fell on him. "I know you're going to ask me next, but I just carve logs as a hobby. My skills are nowhere near what they'd need to be."

Crestfallen, I wrung my hands. "Well, I'm out of ideas. Unless you want a sleigh made out of ice." I managed a weak chuckle. "I don't suppose your husband would enjoy having his behind frozen during his entire journey."

Clara's face brightened for the first time since arriving at the awards event. "What did you just say?"

I began to repeat myself until I felt the weight of her gaze and realized she didn't get the joke. "I wasn't being serious," I defended.

"That's actually a great idea," Wyatt chimed in.

I shot him a death glare. "You don't even know if I could do it or not."

"Yes, I do." He crossed the floor until he stood in front of me. Taking my hands in his, he turned them over. "I've seen what you can do in person and it's absolutely unlike anything anyone else can achieve."

Panic rose in my chest. "You don't know that. All I've done so far is a few glasses and added the water stuff with your bear. Nothing about any of that says that I could craft an entire sleigh, let alone the one that Santa might use."

Clara approached me. "I saw the sculpture with the fish, and I think it's absolutely incredible and very special."

I would have been embarrassed by the compliment if I weren't so freaked out over the sudden expectations resting on my shoulders. "Thanks. But I—"

"The decision is completely up to you, Rory," she interrupted. "If you're truly uncertain that you could do the job, then you can choose not to."

"And be the cause of cancelling Christmas for everyone?" It took great effort to maintain a level of composure and not fall to pieces in front of everyone else.

Mrs. Claus brushed past Wyatt and placed a hand on my

shoulder. "No, Wren is to blame for what happened to the sleigh. You're the reason we have a sliver of a chance to fix things."

I sniffed a couple of times before managing to speak again. "How do you know I could actually do it?"

"Because I've watched you grow in such a short amount of time," she answered. "You came here because you thought you could escape your life. Instead, you've taken bold steps to actually live it. That's why you were able to create the beauty that you did."

I tugged my hands out of Wyatt's grasp and held both out in front of me, staring at them. "But how do I know my magic won't screw things up. It's been broken for so long I don't know if I could trust it."

Clara tilted her head. "Your magic was never broken. Maybe bent a little from doubting yourself. But never broken."

I started to protest and refuse the task she required. But something deep inside of me knew that if I could just trust myself, I could do it. "Maybe," I uttered.

Amos stepped closer to me. "If it helps, I think you should know that I believe in you."

"Same goes for me," Rocky rasped from behind Mrs. Claus, raising his hand in the air.

Nutty scuttled up my body until he perched on my shoulder. "Yeah, yeah, me, too." He kissed my cheek once before scampering back down.

"You already know where I stand." Clara's smile beamed at me with confidence.

I glanced around at everyone, my insides warm and a little gooey from their belief in me. Even though I guessed the answer of the only person left in the room who hadn't added his two cents yet, I still needed to hear the words.

"Wyatt?" I barely squeaked out.

He took my hand and tugged me towards him, catching me against his strong body and encircling his arms around me. "I think you know I'm absolutely crazy about you. Me and my bear have fallen hard for the strong, determined woman you are."

I hid my face against his chest. "I think I'm falling for you, too."

His chuckle reverberated against my cheek. "Think?"

I couldn't bring myself to say anything deeper with my friends listening to everything we said to each other.

Wyatt stopped hugging me and gently pushed me back so he could look me in the eyes. "I could give you a big pep talk about how we all think you can do it, but the only one who really knows whether or not you can is you. Whatever decision you make, I will be right by your side, supporting you."

"You ain't the only one." Amos reached out to touch my arm. "I'm on Team Humbug's side."

Rocky maneuvered closer and leaned his massive body over, thumping his gigantic hand on my back hard enough to knock a little of my breath out of me. Nutty threw his body against my leg and hugged me about my ankle.

Clara couldn't help but laugh at the odd spectacle we created. "All we need to know now is your decision. What's it going to be, Rory?"

I stared into Wyatt's eyes, reveling in the absolute adoration and faith reflected back at me. Taking in a deep breath, I let it out and made up my mind. "I guess I'll give it a try."

A LARGE CROWD gathered around where Clara had led me outside. The added attention did nothing to calm the nerves jangling inside me.

"Do we really need an audience?" I murmured to her as she stood next to me.

"Actually, they'll be helpful," she said. "Santa's sleigh runs on Christmas spirit. You'll need all of their joy and belief in the season to supercharge your work." She took the time to wave at everyone with a bright smile, and the energy of their enthusiastic response crashed over me like a wave on the beach.

I danced from foot to foot, nervous about what came next. "Okay, so how is this going to work?"

Mrs. Claus refused to take the lead and make all the decisions. "I don't know. I said I would help get you started, but from there, it's all up to you."

I held up the sleigh in its miniaturized form, studying every detail with intent. "I think I can get the basic shape if we form a large block of ice and then let me sculpt it from there," I proposed.

Rubbing her hands together in eagerness, Clara said, "One block of ice coming up."

Combining our magic, we created one large hunk of shimmering ice. But unlike the ones found floating in the bay, this one contained a slight mystical glow inside of its very essence.

I wiped a bead of sweat off my brow as I stood back looking at the raw material. Clara carried the tiny sleigh back to me and held it as I planned how to mold the frozen water into the closest form possible to the original.

Vale and her parents joined the rest of the Humbugs, standing at the front of the crowd. All of them cheering me on was the only thing that kept thoughts of running away at bay. Wyatt's eyes glowed as he watched me, but they also held strong emotions that bolstered my confidence.

As I bit my lip, my stomach did flip-flops over the humongous task in front of me. "Here's hoping I don't screw it up."

Clara slapped me on my back. "The good news is that if you do, we can start over again. Your mistakes don't have to define you, Rory. So, the only thing you can do is to try and do your best."

I cracked my neck from side to side and stepped up to the massive block of ice. Holding a picture in my mind of the sleigh, I drew in a calming breath and called on both my fire and ice magic to forge, melt, and mold the frozen chunk into the desired shape.

The roar of the crowd died down as they watched each of my decisions and movements. As the form began to resemble the familiar object, murmurs of *oohs* and *ahhs* rose in the air.

After a tense hour of work, I finished the chassis of the sleigh, complete with seats and storage area for the sack full of presents that Santa carried. Although it remained a bit plain, I wanted to make sure I got the runner mechanisms at the bottom correct so the big man could have a steady way to take off and land without worry.

"I can help you with that," Clara offered, adding her magic into the mix.

We spoke to each other to coordinate our efforts and make sure the rails were formed equally. It took almost another hour to melt the ice down in places while bolstering it back up for support in others. I stood up to stretch after crouching and kneeling for longer than I'd expected. Circling around the work we'd finished, Clara and I surveyed the runners.

"How do we know they'll hold?" I asked her.

With a mischievous glint in her eyes, she ran at the sleigh

and hopped in before I could stop her. She paused for a moment to make sure the whole thing didn't collapse and then threw her hands in the air in triumph. The whole audience burst into cheers and applause, and the slight glow from inside all of the ice sparkled a little more in response.

She jumped up and down a few times. "Seems sturdy enough to me. So, can we declare the task done?"

Now that the basic form was complete, I had a few embellishments I wanted to add. "Not quite."

Using my fire and ice powers, I added small details into the ice. I molded a fancier swirl to the front of the runners and contoured some of the edges. And along the main surface of the sleigh, instead of painted on green and gold filigree like the original had, I etched in snowflakes that grew in size from the front to the back. With a little extra oomph, I boosted the lights from inside to dance and dazzle like the Northern Lights. That final addition made it look like the sleigh was in motion even though it sat still in front of everyone.

The crowd grew quiet as Clara held up her hands. "Okay, Rory. What about now? Is the sleigh finished?"

Taking one last look, I couldn't help the smile that grew on my face. Never in my life would I have guessed I could do anything as beautiful or important as recreate Santa's sleigh.

I nodded in satisfaction. "It's finished."

The crowd whooped and cheered, the chaotic roar ringing in my ears. All of my friends rushed over to me and passed me from person to squirrel to troll to elf, hugging me tight and congratulating me.

Wyatt waited his turn, his eyes blazing once again. He wrapped me into a massive embrace and lifted me off my feet.

I tapped him on his back. "Your bear hug might break me," I wheezed.

He let me down with a loud guffaw. "I doubt anything could do that. But it's nice to know you finally figured that out on your own. Good job, Rory." Planting a warm kiss on my cheek, he released me so I could continue receiving accolades from the throng of excited onlookers.

The more everyone expressed their enthusiasm, the more it activated the holiday spirit of the ice sleigh. After a very quick inspection of her own, Clara stood in the front of the sleigh once again.

She held up her hands to garner attention. "I just want to give special thanks to Aurora Hart for sharing her magic with all of us. Let's give her a round of applause.

Clapping erupted through the whole crowd, and I shook my head. "The praise shouldn't be just for me. I couldn't have done this without everyone believing in me." Glancing around at the rest of the Humbugs, my heart pounded hard in my chest. But this time, instead of nervous doubt, love and appreciation fueled it.

Clara nodded with pride. "Very well. Because of Rory and all the rest of you in Holiday Haven, we can be assured that this Christmas will be the best one yet."

With a flourish of her hand, a light, sparkling snow that smelled and tasted like peppermint fell all around us. Instead of shying away from the sweetness, I relished it, giggling as it melted in my mouth.

Amos rubbed my arm. "You know, I haven't had this much fun in years."

"Does that mean you might actually be looking forward to Christmas?" Wyatt teased.

The older man thought about it for a second, rubbing the stubble on his chin. "You know, I just might. What about the rest of you Humbugs?"

I didn't need to echo the rest of them to know that from here on out, Christmas would be my favorite time of the year.

Epilogue

ale and I sat in her bedroom, getting ready for the Yule Ball. After all of the excitement with Wren and Santa's sleigh, I'd had very little time to pull myself together for the event. But she had it all in hand, helping me book an emergency appointment with Vivienne at Silver & Gold Garments after hours to choose a dress.

"Keep your eyes closed," my best friend demanded. She brushed more makeup onto my eyelids.

It took so much effort not to fidget as she perfected my look. I had never been that into dressing up, not that I'd had a whole lot of occasions to do so in prior years. Tonight would hold many firsts for me, and I could hardly be expected to sit still with all of the excitement and anticipation.

"There," Vale declared, stepping back to admire her work. "Now all you need is a little lip stain, and you'll be perfect. But first, let's get your dress on. I'll have to get Mama since she knows how to tighten the corset."

After a few tense moments, Vale and her mother helped me step into the dress and pull it up. The sleeveless top made of dark navy-blue velvet hugged my body from my chest to my waist. The material changed into something lighter and flowing as the colors morphed from dark blue into ombre colors that ended in light gray. Whenever I moved, it looked as if the colors shifted with me. At the store, Vivienne had called it the Aurora Borealis effect. The second I'd tried it on, I knew it was meant to be mine.

"You look absolutely regal with your hair all done up like that. And your makeup is flawless," Aster declared.

"Thanks to your talented daughter," I added.

Vale's cheeks reddened a bit. "I better get my dress on, too."

My friend would have to get over the embarrassment of receiving compliments. Since Yuletide Yummies lost its owner, the store would have become defunct. However, through the encouragement of the Humbugs and by accepting a loan from her parents, Vale had become the proud new owner.

She twirled in her berry red dress. "What do you think?"

"I think it suits the new owner of Sugarplum's perfectly," I said with a wink.

Vale placed a hand on her hip. "I told you I didn't know whether or not I was going to change the name of the shop."

"But you've taken the concept of sweets to a whole other level now. Instead of just having the baked goods, now you're featuring all the candies you've been perfecting for years. I think that store deserves your name," I insisted.

Aster fixed a matching bow into her daughter's hair. "I agree with Rory."

"But I'm not the sole owner. With all of the elves who used to work for Wren now having a piece of the business, it doesn't feel right to call it Sugarplum's." Vale frowned.

I tweaked the end of her nose. "This is a conversation that can wait for later." I had every intention to convince her to own her awesomeness later.

Jingle knocked on the door. "Is everyone decent? Your escorts are here to pick you up."

"Come in, Papa," Vale called out.

Her father opened the door and gawked at the two of us. "My goodness, if I'd known there were two stars shining as brilliant as the both of you, I would have worn some sunglasses. You two try not to break too many hearts tonight."

There was only one man's heart I was interested in, and I couldn't wait to see his reaction to my getup. "Thank you, Mr. Sugarplum."

Vale kissed her father's cheek. "Don't wait up for me."

"Oh, it might be the other way around. Your mother and I will be joining all of you later. As I recall, my Aster does like to dance until dawn every Yule Ball." He chuckled as his wife enjoyed his flirting.

Vale and I tied some heat-charmed capes around our necks and took careful steps down the stairs and outside the Gingerbread General Store. A large wooden sleigh waited for us right out front. Rocky and Amos got out of their seats. Wyatt waited for me with his hands folded in front of him. His eyes glowed the second he caught sight of me.

"You look absolutely wonderful," he declared as he escorted both Vale and me to the sleigh.

"Nutty, get your furry little behind out of the way," Amos scolded. "And brush the nutshells off the seat."

Rocky held out his hand to help my friend and me step up into the magical vehicle. Nutty did his best to get rid of his mess, but most of it landed on the floor of the sleigh.

"All you boys clean up real nice," I complimented.

Wyatt adjusted a warm blanket over the two of us. He sat on my right side while Rocky climbed into the back seat with Nutty. Amos called forth a little of his magic to get the sleigh moving.

We arrived at the venue and waited until we could pull our ride up to the front doors. Walking into the place together, we took in the charm of the decorations and the general merriment all at once.

Vale took Rocky and Amos's hands. With a little bob of her head and a whistle to Nutty, she flashed a knowing smile at me. "Come on. Let's go find some refreshments."

I untied the cloak from the nape of my neck and whirled it off my shoulders. Wyatt's audible gasp and glowing eyes answered my question of whether or not he would approve.

"You look..." His admiring eyes roamed over me from head to toe more than once. "I'm at a loss for words here."

I acted like his tie needed straightening, stepping closer to him. "Well, that's a trick I'll have to remember. How to stun a bear into silence."

He leaned in closer and whispered in my ear. "I'm gonna be fighting with my animal all night to remain a good Southern gentleman and mind my manners."

A warm shiver ran down my body. "Well, I hope you don't mind them *all* of the night."

He offered me his arm, and I took it, allowing him to escort me further into the magical setting. It took a few minutes to find the other members of our group, and several people stopped us to congratulate me or to talk about wanting to book my services.

Amos had given me a little office space at the back of Pine & Dandy to start my own ice sculpting business. After all the attention the sleigh received, I had so many bookings that I might need to hire an assistant in the new year just to keep up with my schedule. Of course, I made sure Cora was my very first customer.

I almost tripped over Nutty as he scampered underneath my feet, holding onto two nuts I hoped he'd taken from the refreshments area rather than snatching them off of someone's plate.

"It was really generous of you to get your roommate's probation fulfilled as well as your own," Wyatt said as he navigated me through all the small groups milling about the perimeter.

"Well, I think Clara's a softie when it comes to law enforcement. As long as Nutty can stop his habit of stealing and buy his nuts with his Kringle credit, then he'll be fine." I couldn't help but doubt his ability to stay on the straight and narrow forever, but if he did get into trouble, I'd be there to help him out.

"All the attention your work has brought to Holiday Haven has been more than profitable for everyone. You really are an incredible woman," he praised.

I fluttered my eyelashes at him and faked a Southern accent. "Why, kind sir, don't you know that flattery's gonna get you everywhere tonight?"

His deep chuckle vibrated through me. "A man can only hope," he teased.

Instead of guiding me over to a table with my friends, he brought me to the center of the dance floor. Taking my hand in his, he whirled me away from him before tugging lightly and bringing me back into his gentle arms. With expert rhythm, he led me around the dance floor like a pro.

"Where did you learn moves like this?" I asked, falling a little more for him.

He held one hand out from us while he gripped the other around my waist. "My grandpappy and meemaw gave me lessons as I was growing up. He always said if I ever wanted a happy marriage, I'd better learn how to dance through life together."

I swallowed hard. "Marriage, huh?"

Guiding me in another skillful twirl away and then back

to him, he held me tight against him. "Don't worry, I'm willing to take the time to truly get to know each other before talking too much about our future."

Instead of my usual instincts to run for the high hills, butterflies took flight in my stomach and a warm sensation filled me up.

"I got a message from Clara today," I said, changing the subject as fast as possible.

He shook his head with a slight grin at my maneuver. "What did Mrs. Claus say?"

"She said that with all of the attention that spread on the Winternet that the sleigh was completely charged with enough spirit to last the whole night. And that Santa had given it a nickname," I added.

Wyatt raised an eyebrow at me. "How mad would you be if I already knew what it was?"

I gawped at him. "You do? How?"

"Let's just say the jolly man got a little loose with his tongue when I made a special delivery of my newest batch of moonshine to him the other day." The music started to come to an end, and he held on tight as he lowered me into a dip.

"So, what name did ol' Santa tell you he christened the sleigh?" I challenged, looking up at my date.

He brought me back to standing upright first before answering. "Aurora's Heart. He really likes how it shines like the Northern Lights. Said it was a masterful touch."

When I'd read that name in Clara's message, a surge of pride had rooted in my chest and warmed me anytime a little of my old doubt resurfaced.

"I thought it was a nice play on my actual name," I admitted.

Another song began, and Wyatt asked if I'd like to stay. After I said yes, he showed me even more of his smooth moves. "As far as I'm concerned, I'm more partial to the real thing. Kinda hoping I can win it in the long run."

I was enjoying the flirting game too much to tell him that he already had. "We'll have to see. Depends on what you get me for Christmas."

"So, now you're into the holiday spirit?" he asked.

"Yeah, yeah," I teased, mimicking my furry little roommate. "I think looking forward to the season will give me something to run towards every year."

He drew me in close, and I laid my head against his chest. "As long as you're running there with me, I'm happy," he rumbled.

"Hey, don't hog the dance floor," Amos groused. He led Vale to an available spot next to us. "You're not the only one with moves."

A tall lady clung onto Rocky's huge bicep as he joined us. Nutty grasped a nutcracker that was bigger than him and pounced around the floor out of rhythm to the music.

"Happy holidays, you Humbugs," I called out to all of them.

My heart warmed at their instant reply. "Happy Holidays!"

The End

A Note from Bella -

Thank you so much for reading *Sleigh Spells,* and please consider submitting a review! Read more adventures with Rory, Nutty, and the other Humbugs in *Cheery Charms*! And keep reading for a fun bonus story - *A Humbug Holiday*!

I hope you will enjoy the other Winter Witches of Holiday Haven stories as well:

Peppermint Pixies by Danielle Garrett
Jolly Jinxes by J. L. Collins
Holiday Hijinks by Elle Adams
Solstice Spirits by Erin Johnson

JOIN us in our reader group - The Coffee Cauldron

Cora's Brown Sugar Poundcake

INGREDIENTS

- 2 C. Light Brown Sugar
- 1 1/2 C. Butter
- 3 C. Flour
- 1/2 t. Baking Powder
- 1 t. Vanilla
- 1 C. White Sugar

5 Large Eggs
1 C. Milk
1/2 t. Salt

INSTRUCTIONS

Cream sugar and butter. Add eggs one at a time, beating after each addition. Sift dry ingredients together. Add alternately with milk while mixing. Add vanilla and stir. Bake in a greased bundt pan for approximately one hour at 350 degrees.

FROSTING

6 T. Butter
1/4 C. Light Cream
1 C. Brown Sugar

Bring to a boil. Let cool slightly before pouring over cake to help it "set up."

A HUMBUG HOLIDAY

Introduction

Have yourself a very Merry Witchmas in Holiday Haven, where the magic and mystery of Christmas is *snow* joke!

A Humbug Holiday is an extension of Sleigh Spells! It takes place right after it ends.

Now that Aurora Hart has received the gift of a second chance on her life, she is ready to take it on full force. However, this is the very first Christmas where she has friends to celebrate with. A little lost as to what to do, she is willing to take on the challenge to enjoy the holiday to the fullest with her fellow Humbugs!

Chapter One

When the band brought their rendition of "Rockin' Around the Christmas Tree" to a cool rockabilly end, all of us cheered and clapped, drawing in heavy breaths from tearing up the dance floor together.

Amos wiped his brow with a handkerchief. "Whoo, I think I'll sit out the next one." He grabbed his back as a joke. "As the elder statesman of our group, I have earned the right to say what I'm gonna say. I'm gettin' too old for this."

Rocky chuckled and placed a large hand on the older man's back. "I think you move just fine."

Vale bumped my hip with hers. "Okay, it's official. I'm declaring this year's Yule Ball the best ever!"

I giggled as I nudged her back. "As it's my first one, I totally agree!"

Wyatt stood across from me, semi-listening to Clarence talk about something but keeping a close watch on my every move. I winked at him just to watch his reaction. He flashed a very smoldering glance at me that turned my knees into jelly.

"Uh, has anyone seen Nutty?" Amos asked.

His question snapped me out of my flirtations with the bear shifter. "I thought he was right here with us."

The band started playing again, the notes of the slow song rising in the air. People around us coupled up, and Wyatt crooked his finger at me to join him.

I closed the distance between us but stiffened when his arms encircled around me to lead me in a dance. "Nutty's missing," I told him.

His face turned from flirty to serious in a second. "Really? I thought he was right here with us." He searched the floor area around us.

Not that we needed to act as the squirrel's babysitter, but none of us could deny that our little friend tended to get himself into a whole heap of trouble if left to his own devices for too long.

I addressed the rest of our group. "If you were Nutty, where would you be?"

We all looked at each other, and at the same time, we answered in unison, "The refreshments tables."

I smacked my forehead with my hand. "I guess as his roommate, I'll take on the responsibility to retrieve him." If we didn't stop him from eating everything nut-flavored, there might not be any left for anyone else at the ball.

"I'll go with you," Wyatt volunteered, offering me his arm.

I weaved my hand around his muscular tricep and walked next to the handsome shifter with great pride. We didn't make it very far before I felt someone tug on my free arm.

"Excuse me, Miss Aurora." An older woman wearing a silvery blue gown with a sequined pattern of stars all over it grinned up at me. "I was wondering if you could make me something special to put in front of my house."

Her friend noticed us talking to each other and scrambled over to join us, moving faster than I'd expect a lady with a cane would be able to maneuver. "No way, Hester. I was going to ask the sleigh maker to do something for *my* house. You stole my idea."

"You snooze, you lose, Edith," the first woman taunted. She turned back to me, still gripping my arm. "So, how about it? If you could do a rush job, I'd be willing to pay extra."

"Uhhh," I drew out, looking at Wyatt for help.

He shrugged back at me, a slight smug grin on his face his only answer.

"I'll have to check my schedule," I lied, knowing I was already overbooked for my time before the big holiday. "Right now, we need to find our friend."

Wyatt and I made it about ten steps away from that point before someone else accosted me. It still shocked me how much my life had changed in such a short time. I'd helped create a new sleigh for Santa because he needed it. I would never have guessed that my public display at the Seasonal Spirit Awards would change the trajectory of my life to where people sought me out instead of shunning me.

A line had started to form behind the polite man trying to ask me for a new commission. I stood stock still, torn between not wanting to lose potential customers for my burgeoning business and needing to make sure my felonious roommate wasn't doing something that might put him back on probation after I'd arranged with Mrs. Claus to commute his sentence.

Wyatt placed his hand on top of mine. "I'll go make sure our buddy's fine." He winked at me as he removed my hand from his arm. "I'll be back to rescue you in a tick."

"She's no damsel in distress," Cora called out as she rushed over to join me. "Go do what you need to do, Mr. Berenger. Leave this to us women."

"Thanks," I uttered to her out of the side of my mouth. "I'm not exactly sure what to do."

"I do." She cleared her throat. "Ladies and gentlemen, we're so glad that you're interested in Miss Hart's incredible talents. As tonight is the Yule Ball, you can understand that she might want to enjoy the festivities."

"But I want to make sure we get one of her original pieces," the man in the front insisted. "My wife had her heart set on it."

Several of the others behind him piped up how much they wanted me to make something for them as well—a couple of them offering to double my fee, which started a bit of a weird bidding war.

"What do I do?" I asked Cora. "I don't want to turn them away, but I've already got so many appointments booked right now that I know of. How am I supposed to accept even more clients when I can't think beyond a week or so in advance?"

"Hold onto your big-girl britches, cupcake," she responded, rubbing her hands together. "I'm gonna help you make a fortune."

"I don't know about all that—"

"Listen up!" Cora shouted, ignoring my own doubts. "Find a piece of paper and write down your contact information. Or you can wait like civilized people and visit her during her office hours at..." she paused and stared at me to give the pertinent information.

"Pine & Dandy," I finished, tugging on the sleeve to Cora's pretty dress to pull her aside. "But I'm not there all the time."

"That's fine. I'm happy to act as your assistant and make the appointments for you," she offered with a smile.

"You would do that for me? Why?" I asked, too bowled over to comprehend what was happening.

"Because you clearly need the help." She waved her hand at the people scrambling to find something to write on. "Plus, it'll give me something to do again. Retirement is for the birds. I can do my knitting at Amos's place just as easily as I can at home. And getting an opportunity to give that old coot a run for his money on a regular basis will be entertaining as well."

"Wow. Thanks, I guess." I couldn't help the relieved smile that spread on my face.

It really dawned on me that I had a viable business, and now I had my very own employee. That thought gave way to another one.

"Wait, how much should I be paying you for a salary?" I asked.

She tapped her forefinger against her berry-stained lips. "Let's see. I think I could agree to the job for the hefty sum of one custom piece from you every month."

"That's it? That's all you want?" I lifted one eyebrow at her, unable to accept that anyone would be that generous in real life.

She stuck out her hand. "Take it or leave it."

"Oh, I'll take it," I said, shaking on the deal as fast as possible. "But it won't sit well with me to make money and not pay you something."

Cora shrugged. "Since I don't need anything, why don't you set aside an amount you find fair every month and donate it to a worthy cause."

Her idea almost made me cry. "That sounds...wonderful."

"Good." She patted my arm. "Now, why don't you go find your handsome man and drag him to the dance floor. I'll gather all the necessary information and then meet you at Pine & Dandy tomorrow morning."

"Sounds absolutely amazing. Enjoy your evening," I declared, rushing away to find Wyatt and tell him the awesome news.

Once I reached the refreshments area, I searched around the tables but didn't see him or my squirrel roommate. I felt a slight tug on the skirt of my dress and turned around. Two of the elves that I'd worked with at Yuletide Yummies stood behind me.

"Excuse me, Aurora," Pepper said with a smile. "We wanted to tell you that we really like what you do."

I grinned back at her. "Oh, thank you so much."

"And we're so glad you helped to get rid of Ms. Warbler," Ginger added with a gleeful smirk. "She wasn't fun to work for."

I knew that when Vale took over the shop, she'd arranged for the elves who had been her colleagues there to buy into the business and get a share of the profits if they wanted to stay. All of them did so.

"I'll bet Yuletide Yummies is a much better workplace now," I said.

Pepper swallowed her sip of punch. "Oh, yes! We like Vale. She even lets us come up with our own things to bake and sell."

"You should come in and try our gingerbread cookies again," insisted Ginger. "Now we're using *my* recipe, which is a lot more flavorful and less like cardboard."

"I definitely will," I promised. "In fact, maybe I'll start putting in some regular orders to give to my customers as a thank-you after I finish their sculptures." I'd have to remember to tell Cora my idea in the morning.

"By the way, you and that bear of a guy make a cute couple." Pepper nudged Ginger, and the two elves tittered to each other. "He's a tall drink of handsome."

My cheeks heated. "I think so. Have either of you seen him around? He was here not too long ago."

Pepper pointed at a side door nearby. "I saw him go out that way."

"Thank you both so much," I said, stealing a sugar cookie

decorated like an ugly Christmas sweater. Winking at the two friends, I headed towards the door.

A cold wind blasted against me the second I left the ballroom, and I shivered. Snow covered the veranda, and I stepped as carefully as I could in my heels. Wyatt stood with his back to me, his hands gripping the railing.

"Hey," I uttered, guessing he could hear me with his heightened shifter abilities.

Wyatt turned, and the second he caught sight of me, he rushed over. "You must be absolutely freezing." He shrugged out of his coat and wrapped it around me. "There."

"But won't you freeze?" I asked, trying to hide the chattering of my teeth.

"Nah. My bear genes keep me warm enough." For good measure, he pulled me closer to his body.

I nuzzled into his chest and absorbed his natural warmth. "Mmm, I could get used to this."

He placed his arms around me, rubbing my back. "So could I."

We held onto each other under the hush of the moon and stars. When we could hear the beginning of a slow song being played by the band inside, he rocked me back and forth a little. I enjoyed our brief moment together until the night air became too much for me to bear.

"Why did you come out here?" I asked, glancing up.

"I needed a second alone," he replied. "Seeing you getting mobbed by all those people riled up my animal."

I tried to understand what he meant. "You didn't want all of them talking to me?"

"No, that's not what I mean." He pulled back from me and sighed. "My bear was getting overly protective of you, and I needed to come out here and get him to calm down a bit."

"Why was your bear being protective?" I asked. "Nothing about me was in danger. Other than maybe my future time."

Wyatt rubbed the back of his head. "I can explain, but I'm afraid to scare you away."

I pulled on his arm and drew his hand to hold in mine. "Try me."

He drew in a big breath and let it out, a billow of steam blowing around his face. "When someone like me gets attached to another person in a...romantic sense...then a part of what comes with that is a sense to make sure that person will always be okay."

It took me a second to comprehend his words. "Are you saying that your bear has kind of chosen me as a person he wants to take care of?"

His fingers linked through mine. "Yes. And not just my bear. I choose you, Aurora Hart."

A goofy grin of pure happiness settled on my face. "Oh."

He lifted one eyebrow. "What does *oh* mean?"

I giggled. "I think it means I pick you, too."

Happiness radiated out of the big bear of a man. "You do?" He lifted my hand to his lips and planted a kiss on my knuckles.

"I thought you already knew that," I teased, the heat of affection rising in my body and warming me from the inside out.

"Well, we never really had the official conversation about it, and then things got a little crazy these past few days." He cradled my cheek with his other hand.

I leaned into his touch. "Then let's make this official. I, Aurora Hart, choose you, Wyatt Berenger, to be my boyfriend." Standing on my tiptoes, I sealed our relationship status with a quick peck on his lips.

"Oh, I think we can do better than that." His strong arms wrapped around me, and he planted his mouth against mine.

I lost myself in our intimate embrace until I heard a bunch of muted clapping. When I broke away from the kiss, I turned and found all of our friends with their faces and noses pressed up against the window, watching us from inside. They whooped and hollered at us.

Wyatt's low chuckle reverberated through me as he held me close while walking me back inside. Once we entered the warm room, I handed him back his jacket. Hand in hand, we joined our friends.

"Don't all of you have something better to do than stare at us?" I teased.

"Nope." Amos chuckled with great mirth. "If ya don't want any attention, don't go kissin' in public!"

Vale bounced over to me. "We weren't there to spy on you. At least, not at first. I was asking everybody if they wanted to participate in a gift exchange for Christmas."

"And I was in the middle of trying to tell her that the whole point of being a Humbug was that we don't do Christmas," Amos defended. "But then Rocky saw the two of you smooching through the window, and we all had a lookieloo."

Maybe Wyatt's kisses had melted my heart or maybe the excitement of the whole night got to me, but whatever the reason, a warm, fuzzy feeling buzzed through my veins.

"I think a gift exchange would be a lot of fun," I said, earning a couple of groans in response.

"I heard Mama and Papa call it being a Secret Santa," Vale continued. "We put our individual names in a bowl, and then each of us pulls out the name of the person we get a gift for."

Clarence nodded in approval. "Since we are short on time before the day itself, this might be the best scheme to be able to procure a gift in time. It seems the ladies are in. What say the rest of you gentlemen?"

Rocky raised his finger. "I vote yes."

"Yeah, yeah, I'm in." Rocky jumped up and down, his tail twitching with animation.

Amos glanced at each one of us. Realizing he was the last holdout, he hung his head. "Fine. I'll do it, but don't expect me to go all out and actually wrap the present or anything."

All of us surrounded him and gave him a mighty group hug until his protests grew too loud to be ignored. Vale ran off to find some paper, pens, and a bowl. Rocky, Clarence, and Nutty ushered a grumpy Amos towards the refreshments to see if a little punch would cheer him up.

Wyatt took me by the hand and led me to the dance floor. He held my right hand tight in his in between our bodies as he rocked us both to the slow rhythms of the song.

"I hope I get your name," he said, smiling down at me. "Although I've already gotten the best present this Christmas."

"What's that?" I asked.

He twirled me away from him and then pulled me back with great skill. Placing a light kiss on my neck, he whispered into my ear, "You."

Chapter Two

Despite all the wishing in the world that I'd get Wyatt's name when I fished in the bowl for our Humbug Secret Santa project, I'd pulled Amos's instead. After my alarm went off, I laid in bed, trying to think of a good gift to get someone who seemed the most reluctant to participate.

My bedroom door cracked open, and I pulled the covers up over my head, knowing what was coming my way. I heard the scampering of my roommate's tiny feet. The light weight of his body hit my bed right between my feet. He scampered up my covered body until he reached my noggin.

"Get. Up. Get. Up," Nutty squeaked as he jumped up and down on my head.

I giggled underneath the quilt. "Too early," I mock complained.

My furry roommate didn't let up. He danced up and down my torso. "Yeah, yeah, but the nice lady says you have lots of appointments to keep today."

Confused, I stopped playing and pulled the blankets off of me. "What lady?"

"I don't know." Nutty sat on top of my chest, grooming his fluffy tail. "But she brought coffee. Said something about working for you."

When Cora had told me she wanted to work as my assistant, I hadn't taken her seriously. I guess that was all going to change starting today.

I yawned and stretched. "Thanks, Nutty."

"Welcome," he chirped, moving to the foot of the bed so I could climb out.

My mouth gaped again with another big yawn. "Hey, whose name did you end up choosing?" I asked.

Nutty scratched behind his ear with his hind leg. "Wyatt. Don't know what to get the big bear."

Even in my morning stupor, a great idea managed to form. "Hey, I ended up with Amos. Would you be willing to switch?"

My squirrel roommate chittered with glee and hopped up and down. "Yeah, yeah, that would be great!" He jumped down from my bed. "Hurry up or your coffee will get cold."

With my excitement of having Wyatt as the person I got to play Secret Santa to, I rushed through my morning routine and got dressed as fast as possible. Ever since I started taking on clients and making money off the ice sculptures I now made, I'd stopped wearing my dour beloved black hoodie. Vale and her mother had helped me pick out some more professional-looking clothes that still matched my personality.

I chose a red sweater with a Fair-Isle pattern that zipped up the front and still had a hoodie to put on over my white turtleneck. I laced up some black boots over my black jeans that were lined with fleece to help keep my feet warm when I worked outside. With quick fingers, I pulled my hair into a side braid, and was just wrapping the hair band around the bottom to secure it when I exited my room.

"About time," Cora exclaimed. She retrieved a to-go cup from the coffee table. "Figured you could use a little fuel this morning after last night."

I couldn't help the smile that beamed on my face at the memories from the ball. "I don't think I've ever been so..."

"Hot and bothered?" the older lady teased. "Me and my friends watched you and your hunky dunky man twirl around on the dance floor. I gotta say, his moves had a lot of us blushing. Just like you are right now."

I took a sip of the hot drink to hide my utter embarrassment. "We had a lot of fun together," I admitted.

Cora snorted. "I'll bet. Well, you can thank your man for your morning treat. I asked him if I should get you a cocoa from the Candy Cane Cafe, and he told me you preferred bitter coffee instead." She scrunched up her face in disgust.

That man would earn an extra kiss from me. Somehow, the knowledge that he knew a small detail like that about me warmed me from the inside out and made my drink all that more delicious.

"I appreciate it. Now, tell me again why you're here so early," I insisted, willing the caffeine to wake my brain up.

She pulled a small notebook out of her purse. "I took down the info of all the people who want you to make them something, and it's a fairly long list. So, I arranged for some of them to come in to do an in-person consultation. The first one starts today in about...twenty minutes."

"What?" I shrieked, almost spilling my drink. "We gotta go if we're going to make it."

"Exactly," Cora reiterated.

"Nutty, I'll see you later," I called out.

His tiny voice squeaked from behind his bedroom door. "Yeah, yeah, have a good day."

Cora and I walked into the main part of town together while she filled me in on some of the gossip from the Yule

Ball. If I ever needed information on any Holiday Haven resident, she would be my personal Google.

"But of course, the big news of last night is that somebody has won the heart of the lone bear shifter." She bumped me with her elbow. "You know, that hot kiss between the two of you broke a few hearts."

I didn't need my hat and scarf to keep me warm. My flaming cheeks were quite enough. I touched my knitted mitten to my face. "Did everyone see us?"

Cora snickered. "Quite a few. If you want a private moment, try not to kiss someone in front of a bank of windows."

Luckily, we turned onto the main street of Holiday Haven, and Cora got distracted by greeting all the last-minute shoppers as we passed them. It took us a few minutes to reach Pine & Dandy.

I patted one of Wyatt's bears guarding the doors on its wooden head. Shielding my eyes from the sun reflecting off the glass front door, I checked inside to see if Amos had already opened the place.

"Typical. He's not here," I said with a sigh, my breath fogging up the glass.

"That man," harrumphed Cora with her hand on her hip. "He could be making so much money if he would just keep regular business hours. I don't suppose he gave you a key?"

I pulled off the mitten on my right hand and wiggled my fingers. "Nope. I think he enjoys making me have to work for it."

Holding my palm in front of the lock, I willed a bit of my magic down my arm. The familiar heat and chill hit my skin, and a glow emanated from underneath my touch. When I pulled back my hand, a small key made of ice stuck out of the mechanism.

"That's a pretty handy skill," my friend said with wide

eyes. "Kinda makes me glad you're using your magic for good these days."

"Me, too," I admitted, turning the ice key and listening for the unlatching of the lock.

It gave way, and I pulled out the key and made it melt into steam in my palm. As I pushed open the door, the bells on it jangled into the darkened room.

"Wish Amos was here," I said as I glanced around at his beautiful handiwork.

"I am," he groused from behind me, surprising both Cora and me. "I love watching you have to break in, you criminal."

"Takes one to know one," I joked back.

He clicked on the overhead lights and then went around the room, turning on the display lamps that highlighted his wooden masterpieces.

I led Cora to the back corner where Amos allowed me to set up a small card table to work from, but found a surprise waiting for me. Instead of the flimsy table I'd borrowed from Wyatt, a simple but beautiful wooden desk waited for me.

"Amos," I exclaimed, running my hands over the satin grain. "What did you do?"

He came over and stood next to me. "The top is made from purpleheart wood and the legs and drawers are walnut," he explained.

Reaching over me, he moved a stack of papers out of the way to show me an emblem laid into the middle. It showed a red-and-orange flame intertwined with a gray, light blue, and white shard of ice.

"Oh my stars." Tears formed in my eyes. "That is so beautiful."

"Amos, my friend." Cora clapped the man on his back. "You have real talent."

He shrugged off her touch and acted like he didn't care. "It's nothing. I took some scraps of wood I had lying around and made it. No big deal." The older man rushed away from us, and I thought I heard a few sniffs as he disappeared into the back room.

"It so is," I countered in a low voice to Cora.

"Contrary to what he wants the world to believe, he really does have a heart inside that cantankerous frame he calls a body," she agreed. "Now, I'm going to run to the Candy Cane and get us both some breakfast. Well, second breakfast for me. First for you." With a wink, she took off.

Amos reappeared, carrying another chair. "I didn't know you'd have someone else with you."

"Cora's volunteered to be my assistant and help me organize orders," I said, staring at a stack of handwritten requests waiting for me to go through. "I definitely need help. This is my first time running anything."

"You'll learn," he reassured me.

The bells on the door jingled again, and a customer walked in. They admired some of Amos's woodwork, but their face lit up when they spotted me.

"Oops. Looks like that might be my first consultation of the day," I said.

"Good luck," Amos wished me, leaving me to sit behind my brand-new desk.

"Thanks again," I called out to him before greeting my customer.

I MANAGED to get a lunch break sometime after one in the afternoon. Amos had given up running his store before noon and had snuck out the back to go to The Break Room. I'd insisted on giving Cora some money to buy herself and her husband some lunch when he stopped in to check on her.

My boots clomped on the sidewalk as I headed to

Yuletide Yummies. When I made it to the windows out front, I admired the new decorations of messy gingerbread houses made by kids during one of Vale's events. Although they weren't as professional as Wren Warbler's gingerbread replica of the town, they had more heart in them. Plus, my friend said the kids loved to bring their parents to the store just so they could show off their house.

Instead of entering through the front, I snuck my way around back and came in through the employee entrance like I used to. Pepper and Ginger greeted me right away. Buttons almost ran into me while carrying a large sack of sugar. He stopped himself in time and glanced up at me through his floppy hair with a grin. Flake and Flippy waved at me from beside the industrial mixer.

"Hey, everyone," I greeted them.

Pepper wiped her hands on her pink-and-white-striped apron. "Vale's out front, if you're looking for her. Hey, you wanna try one of my Merry Meringues?" The elf held out a tray of small meringue treats in various colors. "The yellow ones are ginger, the white ones with red stripes are cinnamon, and the green ones are mint."

"What about the light blue sparkly ones?" I asked, picking one up.

"Snow," Pepper stated with a smile. "Or at least what I think snow should taste like."

I popped the small treat in my mouth where it melted into sugary goodness. "It definitely reminds me of the way the air smells right before a good snowfall. Cool, fresh, and a little sweet. I think you nailed it."

"Thanks, Rory," she beamed.

I pushed my way into the front of the store and found Vale busy putting together a box of her chocolates for a customer. Pride swelled in my chest as I listened to the gushing compliments about the changes to the store.

"You should have changed the name to Sugarplum's," the older lady insisted.

Vale's cheeks turned a light pink with the attention. "Thank you for your vote of confidence. But I've always liked the name Yuletide Yummies. Although now I get to sell my chocolates, too."

The customer paid and walked out very happy. I couldn't help but give my half-elf friend a big squeeze hello. "I've got about thirty minutes left on my break before I have to work on my commissions. Any chance you could come get some food with me at Whet Your Wassail?"

"Absolutely! Give me one moment." My friend untied the apron and disappeared into the back.

While she was gone, someone else walked in. Since I knew how to handle a sale, I helped the new customer select some holiday pastries and cookies before recommending they treat themselves to a small box of Vale's chocolates as well. I finished ringing them up and handing them the bag when Vale returned with Ginger to take over the counter.

"Wow, I should put you on my payroll," Vale said, bumping me with her hip as we walked out the front door.

"Definitely," I replied with a chuckle. "I come at the hefty price of a few of your truffles every day."

She almost stopped walking. "You know, we've been so busy lately that I'm tempted to take you up on your offer."

I grabbed her hand and dragged her forward. "Don't talk to me about being busy. Now that Cora's helping me organize my new business, it looks like I'm barely gonna have time off for Christmas."

By the time we reached Clarence's British-style pub, I'd filled in my friend on the whole morning. We entered the darkened cozy room of the Wassail and looked for our vampire friend.

"Ladies, what a pleasant surprise," Clarence crooned from

behind the bar. "Take your pick of tables, and I'll be right with you."

Neither of us needed to look at menus since we trusted our friend to serve us something tasty. I told Vale all about my new desk that Amos made for me.

"I'll have to drop by to see it in person. He really is very talented and generous, even though it feels like he doesn't want anyone to know that about him," she said.

Clarence placed a half pint of cider in front of Vale and a pint of Holid-Ale on top of a coaster for me. "Who are we talking about?"

"Amos," Vale and I said together.

I told him about my new desk. Clarence pulled a chair from nearby and sat down in between us. "You know that he helped me restore most of the wood in here, right? My place wouldn't look nearly this good without his help."

Glancing around, I admired the details of the dark wood, especially the intricate carvings near the corners. "His work is amazing, but it's hard to imagine him doing it all."

"Oh, he hasn't always been like he is," Vale countered. "He's gotten a little rough around the edges since his wife's passing."

Clarence nodded in agreement. "He really was quite a jolly fellow to be around. It's sad really to see him so down all of the time. That is, until you came around and forced him to partake in life again." He patted my arm.

"Me? I didn't do anything special," I protested.

"Oh, yes you did." Vale set her glass down hard enough that a little cider dribbled down the side of it. "You recognized a group of others that were hurting almost as much as you were and pulled them together like a family."

"It's true," Clarence added. "Separately, all of us had reasons not to like the holidays. And now, we're all ready to celebrate them like others do. Speaking of, has anyone thought about where we're going to gather when we give our gifts?"

Vale and I glanced at each other with startled faces. "You know, I hadn't thought about it," my friend said. "I could ask my parents if we could do it at our place. But I'm afraid it would be very crowded with all of us there."

I snorted. "Nutty's and my place is a shoebox compared to your family's home. And we can't go to Rocky's cave."

"Wyatt has a decent-sized domicile," Clarence said. "Or we could hold it here at the pub. It'll be closed for Christmas Day, so we'd have the entire place to ourselves."

I mulled over those two fine choices, but an idea kept nagging me. "Do you think Amos would hate us if we asked to use his house?"

Vale gasped. "But he refuses to celebrate the holiday there. He's said it before, it hurts too much because his wife was really into Christmas."

"That's the whole point. Maybe if we help him make new memories there, it might heal some of his hurt." I glanced between the silent other two. "Or maybe I'm being too pushy?"

Clarence rubbed the back of his neck. "It could work. Honestly, I would have just spent the day upstairs catching up on football matches on my own if you two hadn't pulled me into your merry band of brothers. Er, people," he corrected himself. "If anyone has a chance at pulling Amos back into the light of life, it's probably you two fine ladies."

Vale and I devoured two baskets of fish and chips while we discussed the best way to go about convincing Amos. By the end of our meal, we decided to meet up after work and confront him at the Break Room. Clarence wished us luck and refused our money for the lunch and drinks. We snuck a big tip underneath our baskets and hightailed it out of there.

Vale stopped in at Pine & Dandy at the end of the day to

check out my desk. She ran her small hand over the fine craftsmanship the same way I had.

"It truly is beautiful," she uttered in awe. Her brow furrowed, and she stamped the floor. "Come on. You and I need to see if we can break through his gruff exterior and get to his ooey gooey center. There's no way that man can make something this beautiful and not have a heart."

I showed her the secret exit from Amos's store that led into Wyatt's bar. Vale held my hand and tugged me forward, determined to succeed on our mission.

We found the usual crowd hanging around. Wyatt perked up the second he caught sight of me, and the butterflies in my stomach took flight at his attention.

"Hey, gorgeous," he called out, pulling one of my ice mugs off the reserved shelf. "You come here for a drink or the company?"

"A little of both," I said, smiling back at him. A quick search of the customers revealed no Amos. "Where's our top Humbug?"

"If you mean Amos, then just wait a few minutes. He's been here all afternoon, and I doubt he'll be leaving anytime soon." Wyatt frowned. "I tried my best not to serve too much to him. I just think this time of year gets him a little down."

Vale climbed onto a barstool and perched. "That's why we're here. Rory and I think we've come up with a plan that might help him out."

Wyatt lifted one eyebrow. "You have, have you? Tell me this brilliant plan of yours."

"We want to ask him if he'll allow us to use his house to do the Secret Santa exchange," I explained with enthusiasm.

Instead of an enthusiastic response, Wyatt stayed unusually quiet.

"You don't think it's a good idea?" I asked him.

He pondered my question for a second. "I think you can lead a horse to water, but you can't force it to drink."

Before I could question him what he meant, Amos entered the room again. "Who are you trying to force to drink? And if they don't want what you're serving, you can give it to me," he slurred.

"Amos, have you been in here drinking all day?" I asked, wondering where the man who'd presented me with the desk had disappeared to.

He waggled a finger at me. "I did my one good deed today. And besides, with all those people coming in and out of my place of business, they all came in to talk to you. Not one of them bought anything of mine."

"That's because you kept disappearing," I said in defense. "I recommended your stuff to every single one of them, but since you were nowhere to be found when they had questions, they couldn't buy anything."

He half sat on a stool and half stood when he didn't wobble on his feet. "You have my permission to sell my stuff anytime you want."

"I have my own job," I replied.

"Well, then tell your secretary she can do it." Amos stuck out his tongue. "That Cora needs to mind her own business anyway. She tried to tell me that she had a single friend she'd like to introduce me to."

Wyatt, Vale, and I all exchanged knowing glances at each other. It was more than likely that Cora's well-intended suggestion at a possible date had sent Amos into a tailspin.

"She didn't mean anything by it. I think Cora is a fixer by nature," I said, approaching the hurting man and putting an arm around his shoulder. "But I think we should probably get some food in you. And maybe a little coffee."

Amos's eyes drooped a little. "I'm not as think as you drunk I am," he slurred again.

"I don't think he should be on his own tonight," Vale said, her words dripping with worry. "And it's definitely not the right time to ask him about his house."

"What about my house?" Amos asked, perking up.

I shook my head. "Don't worry about it for now."

"No, I think you should tell me. Is there something wrong with my house?" he asked, his drunken concern growing.

I looked at Wyatt for a suggestion, but my boyfriend just shrugged at me. "Nothing's wrong with your house. But we were kind of hoping we could do our Secret Santa exchanging of gifts there on Christmas."

Amos leaned away from me. "Is Santa coming to see me at Christmas?"

Vale placed a hand on the man's back to keep him from falling backwards on her. "No, not Santa himself. Just our group. All of us Humbugs."

He snorted. "Humbugs. Like what Scrooge says all the time. He didn't like Christmas either, just like me."

"Yes, but Scrooge has a change of heart in the end," I said, knowing that we weren't going to get anywhere with our friend in the condition he was in.

"Pfft. That stuff only happens in stories." Amos jutted his thumb at his chest. "No heart in here to change."

"Now, that just isn't true," Vale protested.

Amos turned to look at her and stumbled a bit. He closed one eye but kept the other one trained on her. "There. Now there isn't two of you trying to be nice to me."

"I'll bring him back to my place with me," Wyatt declared. He threw the towel he'd been using to wipe down the bar over his shoulder. "Bar's closing in five minutes," he barked to the rest of the patrons in the place.

"You don't have to lose business because of him. We'll get him home," I said.

Amos smiled once and then promptly collapsed at our

feet. Wyatt emerged from behind the bar and rolled our friend over, making sure he hadn't hurt himself in the process.

"I doubt the two of you could carry him the whole way. Plus, I'll make sure he doesn't get into any more trouble." My sweet-hearted boyfriend kissed my cheek. "Sorry we couldn't really spend anytime together tonight."

I sighed. "It's fine. I guess it wasn't such a good idea."

"Now, I never said that. Why don't you leave it to me and see if he has a different answer for you in the morning." Wyatt winked with a sly grin.

"Do you possess some secret powers of persuasion?" I asked.

"I managed to convince you to say yes to being my girlfriend, didn't I?" He wiggled his eyebrows at me.

"True. Before you kissed me, I was totally going to turn you down." Amos groaned from his position on the floor. "But I would highly suggest you make him brush his teeth before trying that tactic on him."

"Ha. Ha. Just for that, you might be getting coal from your Secret Santa." He crouched down and maneuvered Amos into his arms, lifting him up as he stood.

The butterflies in my stomach turned to buzzing wasps of worry. What if Wyatt had pulled my name? I hadn't even figured out what I was going to give him yet.

"Yeah, well, your Secret Santa might hear about that and make sure you get nothing," I awkwardly countered. "Come on, Vale, I'll treat you to a cocoa."

"I'll let you know if anything changes in the morning," Wyatt called out to us as we left.

Vale allowed me to usher her out with great haste. The second we made it outside, she confronted me. "What was that all about?"

"I think Wyatt might have pulled my name for Secret Santa," I said.

"So?"

"So, I traded Nutty for his name. And I just realized, I have *no* clue what to get him," I whined.

My friend hooked her arm through mine. "Then let me treat you to some coffee, and we'll discuss your options."

Arm in arm, we went off on yet another mission. We'd have to wait until tomorrow to figure out what to do about Amos.

Chapter Three

I received a text in the morning from Wyatt for all of the Humbugs to meet him at Amos's house. Nutty and I headed out into the chilly day together, and I listened to my roommate chitter-chatter as he bounced along beside me. Every once in a while, he'd skitter to the side, sniff the ground, and dig a small hole to see if he'd buried a nut there.

When we arrived at the modest but well-kept home, Vale waved at us as she approached from the other direction. "I take it you got the message as well?"

"Us, too," Rocky called out as he walked beside Clarence. "Do you know why?"

I filled the small group in on Vale's and my idea to have the Secret Santa exchange at Amos's place. But after seeing him in the condition our friend was in the previous night, guilt gnawed at my insides.

The front door creaked open and Wyatt stepped outside onto the front porch. "Why don't y'all come in outta the cold. Unless you want to start crooning me with some carols, get your behinds inside."

We shuffled inside, and I glanced around at the clean

interior with wooden accents at every turn. Amos had put a lot of love and work into his place and it showed. However, the floral patterns and softer furniture that complimented all of the woodwork didn't escape my notice.

"I've got coffee and cocoa in the kitchen, plus I scrambled up some eggs and fried some bacon in case any of you are hungry," Wyatt offered. "Grab a plate of food and then meet back in the living room."

He sauntered over to me and I wrapped my arms around his middle, pressing my face into his chest. "Good morning," I murmured.

Wyatt kissed the top of my head. "Morning, although I haven't even made it to bed yet."

I glanced up at him. "You didn't sleep at all last night?"

He chuckled and rubbed my back. "Nope. Our friend needed a lot of help. I'm not sorry for being there for him, though."

I stood on my tiptoes and planted a kiss on his lips. "You're such a good guy."

Wyatt lifted me with ease in his hold and deepened the kiss. "If you knew the thoughts running through my tired brain right now, I'm not so sure you'd think I was good."

I giggled under his intense attention until Clarence reappeared and cleared his throat. Wyatt swatted my butt as I hightailed it to the kitchen to pour myself a much-needed cup of coffee. One lone strip of bacon waited for me, and I stuffed it in my mouth while I scooped out some scrambled eggs on a plate. I grabbed a fork and napkin and headed back into the living room.

All of the available seats were taken, and I contemplated sitting on Wyatt's lap, but the big guy got up from the couch to give me his place despite how exhausted he must be.

"I'll go get Amos, and then we'll have a short talk." My boyfriend disappeared from the room.

Vale shoveled a forkful of eggs in her mouth. "I hope everything's okay."

"I don't think we'd be sitting here eating a casual breakfast if it weren't," I replied, ignoring the little bit of worry still in residence in my gut.

Amos shuffled into the room looking disheveled and unshaven. The pallor of his skin was a bit ashen, and bags drooped under his eyes.

"Did everybody get enough to eat?" he asked, acting like a normal host.

Clarence flashed his fangs with his smile. "We're good, my friend. And how are you this sunny morning?"

Amos grunted. "A bit worse for wear, as I'm sure you all can see." He gestured at his own appearance. "I'd like to apologize for my actions last night. Imbibing too much doesn't excuse poor behavior."

He scratched at the stubble on his face, glancing at me. I smiled back at him. "We've all had rough nights before. Nothing to apologize for. And I really shouldn't have asked you to be the host to all of us for Christmas this year. We should take Clarence up on his offer to do things at his pub."

"I'd be more than happy to have all of you there," the vampire exclaimed.

"That's actually why I asked Wyatt here to have you all come to my place," Amos said. He let out a long sigh. "I know that I'm the biggest Scrooge of the group."

Vale and I exchanged knowing glances while a few others voiced their mock disbelief. The older man snorted at our reactions.

"Well, it's true, and I've taken on that role for far too long. In truth, I've actually had more fun in the past month than in several years." He clapped Wyatt on the back. "After a long talk with this one, I've realized that maybe it's time I take some baby steps to trying a little harder to actually live my life rather than letting every day pass me by."

"That sounds like a healthy plan," Vale chirped.

"Yeah, yeah," agreed Nutty.

Amos took slow steps over to the polished wood mantle over the fireplace. He retrieved a silver photo frame and held it with great care in his hands. "When Mabel was sick, she made me promise not to retreat from life but to live it to its fullest. Especially at Christmas. I'm ashamed to say, if she saw me now, she would give me an earful, I'm sure." His voice wavered as he finished his statement.

Tears welled in my eyes, and Vale sniffed audibly. "Oh, Amos. She was a wonderful woman, and we all miss her."

It took a long moment for Amos to gather his wits. He placed the photo back on the mantle and stroked a finger down the surface of the picture. "Well, what I'm about to say is in honor of my Mabel. I'd be happy to host all of you for Christmas." He swiped his hand across his cheek to catch a stray tear. "Although if we're going to whip this place into shape in time, I'm going to need a little help decorating it."

Wyatt beamed at me from his position behind his friend. I didn't know how he'd done it, but somehow, my bear of a boyfriend must have gotten through to our resident curmudgeon while taking care of him last night. I blew a kiss in his direction, and he chuckled.

Vale and I worked on cleaning up the kitchen while the boys brought down all of the boxes of decorations. It turned out that Mabel had been a huge fan of Christmas, and the amount of stuff to hand up or put out overwhelmed me.

Rocky held up his hand. "I'll take the outdoor decorations."

"I'll help!" Nutty bounded over to the rock troll and clambered up his body to sit on his shoulder.

"I can also assist," Clarence offered.

"That leaves us to handle the interior," I said, putting an arm around my half-elf witchy friend.

Wyatt shrugged on his coat. "I guess I'll go find us a tree."

Vale whipped out her spell phone from her pocket. "Oh, I can get one here in no time." With a couple taps on the screen, she got in touch with her contact. "Crispin? I need to put in a special order and put a rush on it." Her voice trailed off as she walked into another room to talk to her cousin.

Amos pulled himself together and took charge of all of us. He got Rocky and Clarence to carry the boxes of exterior decorations outside. Vale and I dug through the boxes with some of the more precious items to put out on display, making sure to check in with Amos as to where he wanted things.

Crispin arrived within an hour, and he and Wyatt set up a gorgeous Frasier fir in a corner of the living room. Vale's cousin also brought a wreath and some pine swag to hang off the front porch. He even stuck around to help the crew outside with securing the swag and all the lights.

Wyatt got busy weaving lines of colored lights throughout the tree. I opened the box full of ornaments and placed hooks in them before handing each one to Amos. He told me stories about Mabel and him as he filled up all the branches. Although I'd never met the woman, I felt like I got to know a little more about her and a lot more about my friend through each of his memories.

"Wait. Let me open that one." Amos pulled out a smaller red box and pulled off the lid. He peeled away the tissue paper and pulled out a delicate angel made from metal and stained glass.

"That is so beautiful," I remarked, staring at the angel over his shoulder.

"She's been gracing the tops of our trees since we got

married." Amos's fingertips stroked the delicate wings. "Mabel used to use her witchy powers to float her to the top."

I swallowed hard. "I'd be afraid to try that since my magic might freeze or melt it."

Vale approached the melancholy man and touched his shoulder. "I'd be honored to do it, if you'd like."

Amos sniffed a couple of times and nodded. He handed our half-elf half-witch friend the angel. She cradled it in her palms until she summoned energy in her hands. Then, the angel floated out of her grasp until it reached the pinnacle of the tree. With careful deliberation, she settled onto the top branch. The lights that were wrapped around twinkled through the angel's glass skirt, making her look more ethereal.

"I really should thank you guys for pushing me," Amos said, standing in front of the tree and admiring it. "I knew Mabel would have hated the last few Christmases I let pass by, but I just couldn't bring myself to celebrate without her."

Wyatt came over and put a heavy arm around my shoulders. "It's our pleasure, man." An involuntary yawned escaped him.

"I owe you one, Wyatt, for last night. You're a good friend." Amos patted my boyfriend on the arm as he went outside to inspect the outside of his house.

I leaned against Wyatt's solid frame. "We should get you home so you can sleep a little."

"I'll be fine," he lied through another yawn. "Besides, there's a little more I have to do to get my gift ready for Christmas." He winked at me.

Even though Vale and I had come up with several options for gifts to give to Wyatt, I still hadn't settled on a gift for him yet.

"Who are you playing Secret Santa to?" I asked, hoping he wouldn't notice my internal panic.

"Telling you is against the rules. That's the whole *secret* part to the game." He lifted a finger to his lips. "I just hope whoever it is will like the gift."

I let out a nervous chuckle. "I'm sure whoever it is will appreciate anything you put your heart into. Speaking of, I also should work on the finishing touches for the person whose name I pulled."

"I'll walk you out," Wyatt offered.

We admired the handiwork of the others while standing in front of Amos's place. With a little help, the pleasant house had turned into a very festive home.

"Ha!" Amos exclaimed with great glee.

"What has you so amused, my friend," Clarence asked him.

Amos hooked his thumbs through his belt loops. "I was just thinking about how Wren Warbler hated it when I didn't decorate my house. She would have *loved* to see it like this."

All of us broke down in laughter at the thought of the horrid woman who'd almost ruined Christmas for everyone after stealing Santa's sleigh.

Thanks to all of us, the holiday would end up being the best ever. And, unknown to the rest of my friends, my very first time celebrating. Especially with a group of friends I now considered my chosen family.

Chapter Four

I'd visited every single store in Holiday Haven, looking for a present that would fit Wyatt. And I'd still come up empty-handed and even more panicked. It took four of Vale's special chocolate truffles to keep me from the pits of despair. Well, maybe more like six or seven.

"Why don't you make him one of your ice sculptures?" Vale asked as she closed down Yuletide Yummies for the day.

I groaned. "Because that feels like a cop-out. Like he'd be expecting that. I'd already made him a bunch more of the ice mugs for him to use for his customers before we started this whole Secret Santa business. It just feels...unoriginal."

My friend snorted. "I think your ice creations are far from unoriginal. You have no idea how many people ask me if I can get their names moved up on your waiting list when they come in here."

I stared back at her in astonishment. "They do?"

"Uh-huh," she admitted with a grin. "I just tell them to talk to Cora now."

"That woman is the best thing to happen to me. I really should get her something special for Christmas, but she told me not to go to any trouble." I threw up my hands in surrender. "This gift-giving thing is way harder than I ever thought it would be."

Vale switched off the lights to the front of the business and pushed me back into the kitchen. "How do you normally choose gifts for others?"

I glanced around the room at the busy elves cleaning up. Lowering my voice, I answered, "Uh, I've never given gifts before."

Her eyes widened. "Never?"

I didn't care for the pity I saw in her expression. "So, do you have plans for dinner or do you want to hit up the Wassail with me?" I said, changing the subject.

She snapped her fingers. "Oh, frosted sugar cookies, I forgot to tell you. Mama wanted me to invite you over to our place for dinner."

"Well, I'm not turning down some of her home cooking! Hurry up so I can fill up my belly with goodness already," I teased, jumping in to help move things a little faster.

It didn't take us very long to get the place spic-and-span for the next day. Vale waited for all of the others to leave before switching off the lights and locking up. We walked down the street towards the Gingerbread General Store, talking about Amos and his change of heart.

Aster Sugarplum threw her arms around me the second we arrived to the top floor of the store that served as Vale's family home.

"Welcome, Rory," the witch exclaimed. "We're so happy you could join us tonight. Jingle should be up shortly for dinner. Come in and make yourself at home."

It wasn't hard to follow my friend's mother's orders because their place had always felt like what I'd imagined a home to be. All those years of living day to day on my own and peeking in through open windows, I'd created the fantasy place in my head of what having a family might be like. And today, I stood inside a home that fulfilled all my dreams.

Aster brought me a mug of steaming coffee and one of cocoa for her daughter. "Catch me up on why Vale had to rush off this morning."

We sat down and told her everything about our friend and decorating his house. She cried a little, especially when Vale told her about her role in placing the angel at the top of the tree."

"That man deserves some happiness after so much time spent in mourning," Vale's mother said. "I'm glad you two girls pushed him. And that you've been able to find a group of people who maybe needed a little help in their lives as well."

"Us Humbugs have to stick together," I declared, sticking my mug out in front of Vale.

"Hear, hear." She giggled and clinked her glass against mine.

"What are we celebrating," Jingle asked as he came in, making us all titter with laughter again.

Aster served us an amazing roasted chicken with garlic mashed potatoes and a broccoli dish that didn't make me hate vegetables. I stuffed my face until my stomach hurt, and helped clear the table after we'd all finished.

"Let's go into the living room and visit a bit to let things settle before I serve dessert," Vale's mother suggested.

"Good idea, my sweet," Jingle agreed. He sat down in his usual chair, and Vale and I occupied the couch.

My friend didn't stay seated very long. When her mother entered, she popped up and started fussing with the wrapped presents under the tree. She emerged, holding one of them in her hands.

"Here." She held out the present to me. "This is from my parents."

My cheeks blazed. "But I didn't get you anything."

Aster placed a warm hand over mine. "Oh, yes you did. Before you came, our daughter stayed inside her shell far too much. But now, she's absolutely flourished with your friendship. That is a gift that we can never repay."

Vale thrust the present at me again. "Just open it."

The paper covering the box was red with glitter reindeer all over it. I didn't want to ruin it, so I tore at the tape with great care, taking my time.

"Oh, for goodness sake, just rip it off," Vale insisted.

With a little childish glee, I did as she asked, tearing the paper apart with my fingers. I unfolded the tabs of the box and searched through the mess of red, green, and white tissue paper. Several different bags of coffee beans lay inside the large container.

I picked one up and read the label. "Wow. This is absolutely amazing. And way too much."

"No, it's not," Jingle said, beaming a wide grin at me. "I asked the big man what his favorite blends were since I was already putting in an order for him."

I froze in place. "Are you saying that I'll be drinking the same coffee as Santa?"

"Yes, indeedy," Vale's father crowed.

"Thank you so much, Mr. and Mrs. Sugarplum," I gushed.

Vale rolled her eyes. "That's not your entire gift." She crawled under the tree again and dragged out an even bigger box. "Here."

Still a bit embarrassed at receiving such generosity, I tore the paper away to reveal a very nice coffee maker. I traced the picture on the outside of the box. "You really shouldn't have."

Jingle got up from his chair and came over. "This here's supposed to be one of the best. See here where you can put the beans in? It'll grind them for you so the coffee'll be nice and fresh."

"And it's programmable, so you can have it all ready for you by the time you get out of bed," Vale added.

I couldn't find the words to express my gratitude. Not just for the gifts, but also for treating me with such kindness. Unable to speak, I threw my arms around each one of them, trying to convey everything I couldn't say through my hugs. I planted an extra kiss on Vale's cheek.

"Now, let's keep the sweetness going. Who wants a slice of my chocolate Yule log?" her mother asked.

VALE and I walked arm in arm down the street. She had decided we needed a little walk after imbibing in so much good food.

"Did you like your presents?" she asked.

"Very much," I said, nudging her with my elbow. "Although it's a little weird accepting presents, too."

"Well, I hope you having a coffee maker and good coffee doesn't mean you and I won't go get drinks together during the day." She bumped me back, knocking both of us off course a little.

"Never," I promised.

We passed all of the closed shops while we talked. I thought for a moment that she might be taking me to Whet Your Wassail for a little drink. Instead, we kept going until we made it to the town square.

The large community tree decorated by everyone in town towered over us. Vale pulled something that crinkled out of her coat pocket and held it out to me.

"Another gift?" I scolded. "This is way too much, and you're starting to make me feel a little guilty."

"That's the last thing I want you to feel. Because Mama was right." My friend looked up at me with glistening eyes.

"Before you came, I kind of went through the motions of living life. I didn't really look forward to anything. It was a bare-minimum existence, and that's no way to live."

"Me, too, Valey," I said. "There are things I'm ashamed to say I did just to get through every day. But I don't think I can regret what brought me here in the first place. Even if that means I'm really a criminal."

"No, you're a good person who did what she had to do to survive," Vale corrected. "And you're right. I can't regret what brought you to Holiday Haven either."

We hugged each other until she pushed me away and waved the small present at me. "Here. You have to open it."

With a sigh, I acquiesced. I pulled off my mittens with my teeth and worked off the ribbon around the small wrapped object. Not wanting to hurt whatever it was, I took greater care in peeling off the paper.

"Oh, Vale," I exclaimed with great admiration, picking up the gift.

I held a clear angel ornament in front of me. The lights from the Christmas tree twinkled in its body.

"I think I always knew I wanted to get you an ornament ever since the first day we met," my friend said in a quiet tone. "It took me a while to find one that fit you, and I almost busted a gut when I saw Amos's tree topper."

"She's gorgeous." I turned her around, enjoying the flash of light that sparkled.

"Well, I thought it would look a little like your ice sculptures." She poked at it, watching it dangle back and forth. "And then I picked this one because I kind of think of you like *my* angel who came and made my life so much better."

Without hesitation, I wrapped my arms around my friend and gave her the biggest hug. "Thank you."

She kissed my cheek. "So, now that you're a real Holiday Haven resident, you have to hang it on the tree."

I laughed through the tears that fell down my cheeks. "I guess I do."

My friend helped me pick a spot about half way up the tree that had lights hanging right behind it. With a little guidance from Vale, I managed to levitate the ornament to the right place. The angel wavered in the night breeze, the Christmas lights causing the ornament to sparkle like it had magic of its own.

Without knowing it, my half-elf friend had given me the perfect gift. It wasn't big or expensive, but it fit me perfectly. And all of a sudden, a flash of inspiration hit me.

I gasped, startling Vale. "What?" she asked me.

"I know who I need to ask to help me with my gift for Wyatt." I practically danced in place.

My friend clapped with enthusiasm and bounced up and down. "Yay, finally."

I pulled out my spell phone and swiped through my contacts until I found the very special one. "If anyone has access to what would be a perfect gift for someone, it has to be the top residents of the North Pole!"

Chapter Five

The scent of cinnamon, nutmeg, and peppermint filled the air. A spiral of wind and snow filled my small living room. Out of the winter vortex walked Clara Claus, my friend and wife to Santa.

"Hey, Rory. I got your message." She shook off the snowflakes clinging to her hair and pulled her one long braid over her left shoulder. "What can I help you with?"

I handed her a mug of coffee made with my new gift from Vale's family. "I need some help figuring out the perfect gift for Wyatt."

She accepted the drink with a grin. "Thank you, but I don't know why you need my help to figure out what to get your boyfriend."

Her statement shocked me. "You knew about that?"

Clara waved a hand in the air. "Oh, honey, there's very little that goes on here that I don't know about. You're now living in a very tight community. It would be hard for you to sneeze without someone in Garland Gale or Poinsettia Point blessing you for it. Besides, when one of the most desired eligible bachelors goes off the market, believe me—everyone knows about it."

I knew that several of the older ladies admired my boyfriend, but I didn't know I might have made some enemies by us choosing to be together.

Sensing my trepidation, Mrs. Claus attempted to put me at ease. "Oh, it's nothing so dramatic. Honestly, pretty much everyone is happy when a young couple finds happiness with each other."

"It's a very new relationship. My first, actually," I admitted. "And that's why I want to try and get his gift right. I realized last night that what I give him has to come from the heart. But I'm so new to all this gift-giving that I'm afraid of screwing it up."

Clara leaned forward. "And that's where you're wrong. I think you could give that man a hug and he'd be happy about it. It's not about the actual gift as much as in the giving."

"I'm starting to learn that," I said, thinking about Vale's ornament for me.

"Good, that's the first step." She settled back into her place on the couch and took a big sip of coffee.

"But can't you tell me what he'd most like? There must be some book that you and your husband have with a list of things," I begged.

She raised one eyebrow at me. "And would that be getting him something from your heart?"

I slumped into the back of my seat, careful not to spill any coffee. "No, I guess not," I mumbled like a petulant child.

Clara crossed her legs, and I couldn't help but be distracted by her amazing boots. They were dark, but not necessarily black. The color morphed and changed like the night sky. Every once in a while, they would twinkle as if her shoes possessed their own galaxy of stars.

"Trust me, when I was first with Nick, I didn't know what to get him either. I mean, the guy gives gifts to the entire world. What does someone like that want for himself?" She took a slow sip of her drink. "And then I learned to watch. To listen to him, especially when he was talking from in here." She tapped her chest over her heart.

My little bit of worry turned into a deeper anxiety. "But we haven't been together that long at all."

Mrs. Claus shot me a lopsided grin. "Sometimes it doesn't take a lot of time to know when things are right. But it will take effort to get to know one another."

Maybe what I needed to give Wyatt was exactly that. A chance to get to know each other better. But when exactly would I have time to do that? Now that I had Cora organizing my work calendar, I was pretty sure I was booked up for the very foreseeable future.

"Do you think promising him a good date night would be enough?" I asked. Without waiting for an answer, I stood up and paced around. "That feels like something I should put together for him even when it's not Christmas."

"Surely, you didn't come to the conclusion of dating each other without having some sincere talks. Don't panic," Clara insisted. "Let's break this down. What do you know about him?"

I bit my lip as I thought about it. "He's good down to his core. He's willing to risk his life for others. Even when that meant he had to go away from the family that he loved."

Mrs. Claus nodded. "Keep going," she pushed.

"And that he's a bear shifter, although I'm still learning about what that kind of life is like. He told me his bear is really protective of me." I stopped pacing. "Which I kind of like because *nobody* has ever looked out for me like that before."

"Oh, I think you've found plenty of people here who have your back," she replied with a chuckle.

"So, should I be getting a gift for his bear? I'm not even sure what they like to eat. Like, is it even real that bears like honey or is that just in fiction?" I asked.

The smile on Clara's face faltered. "I'm not so sure I would try to go about feeding Wyatt's animal. That's only a part of him. You want something that will fulfill the needs of the whole person—man and bear."

I tapped my mug with my fingernail. "He likes to make moonshine. Maybe he needs a part to help him make it. Or I could find a bunch of ingredients for him to use to infuse it with flavors like I've seen in stores."

Mrs. Claus snapped her fingers. "Now you're onto something. That would probably pique his interest and challenge him in a fun way. And then you can be his test subject for all the different flavors. Heck, my husband would volunteer as well in a heartbeat!"

Maybe I wouldn't fail at this gift-giving after all. "I like it. Although it still doesn't feel totally right." I thought about what Wyatt had told me about why he made moonshine in the first place.

An idea blossomed in my brain, and the buzz of enthusiasm energized me. "Ooh!" I bounced up and down in front of Santa's wife. "I know exactly what to get Wyatt."

Clara leaned forward and placed her mug on the table in front of her. "Tell me. I'm dying to know."

"But the problem is, I don't know how to pull it off," I said to myself. Glancing at my friend sitting in my modest living room, I took a chance. "You're absolutely right."

She flashed a smug smile. "I usually am, but why don't you tell me why that's true right now."

I tapped the left side of my chest. "Because this tells me

that I'm on the right track. But there's one problem that maybe you can help me out with."

Clara clapped her hands together and rubbed them. "Name it."

"I'm gonna need a little transportation assistance."

Chapter Six

With Wyatt's gift all squared away, I got an incredible night's sleep. But as soon as a sliver of light leaked through my curtains, I bolted upright. Today was Christmas! The first one I looked forward to in my entire life!

I bounded out of bed and pulled on my fleece-lined red socks that had white snowflakes on them. I put on my favorite black hoodie to keep me warm, but the night before, I'd secured a decorative brooch on the left side of it. With one click of a switch, tiny lights on the metallic green wreath blinked on and off. If I pressed the button on the side, the brooch played a tinny rendition of "The Twelve Days of Christmas."

My squirrel roommate usually woke me up, but this morning, I was ready to turn the tables on him. I snuck across the space in between our bedrooms and opened his door with great care so it wouldn't creak.

Nutty's little form lay on top of his pillow, all curled up in a tiny ball. Stifling my own giggles, I leaped onto his bed and bounced. "Get. Up. Get. Up," I insisted, mimicking him.

His tiny head lifted up and he opened one eye. "What time is it?" he asked.

"It's Christmas o'clock!" I shouted. "My first one in Holiday Haven, and I intend to enjoy every second of it." I crawled up the bed until I sat next to his pillow.

The little squirrel yawned and scratched his ear with his back paw. "Yeah, yeah, I'm awake."

I stroked his tiny head between his furry ears. "The faster you get up, the sooner you get to open the present I got you."

The mention of a gift spurred my roommate into action. "But you traded me for Wyatt's name. And I thought I took Amos's, not my own."

"That's true," I admitted. "But I couldn't let Christmas go by without getting something for my incredibly awesome roomie."

He climbed my arm until he sat on my shoulder. Placing his little paws on my head to steady himself, he leaned in and gave me a quick peck on the cheek.

"Got you something, too," he chittered.

I pushed myself off his bed. "Come on. Let's go out into our living room where we can exchange our gifts like others do. By a roaring fireplace and near a lit-up Christmas tree."

It took very little of my magic to get a fire going. Still waiting on Nutty and wondering what a squirrel had to do to get ready that took so long, I managed to brew myself a cup of coffee.

I patted the new machine with great affection, knowing how much I loved the people who gave it to me. Maybe that was the benefit of gift-giving. Not in the receiving of things but in being able to enjoy thinking about who the gift comes from.

Nutty bounded out of his bedroom wearing a tiny Santa hat. He sang "Jingle Bells" at the top of his lungs, bounding across the floor to the rhythm of the song. We danced like fools with each other, but since no one saw us, it didn't matter. When we finished, we both lost our breath from laughing so hard.

"Gift time!" I announced, running to my room and carrying out a very large box.

"Yeah, yeah, me first," the excited squirrel declared. He scampered into his room and returned, carrying a golden box with a bow on top that I recognized.

"Oh, Nutty! I hope that's what I think it is." I accepted the gift and pulled off the velvet ribbon holding it together.

At least two dozen of Vale's chocolates were nestled inside. There were so many that I wouldn't even know where to start.

"Knew you would like them. Vale promised me," he said, skittering over to sit beside me. "I picked out the ones with nuts on top of them."

"Did she let you try one?" I asked with a grin.

He nodded, licking his lips. "Of course, but maybe I forgot what they taste like."

I held the box out in front of him. "Why don't we both choose one for each of us."

Nutty didn't need me to insist. He snatched one of the nut-topped chocolates and stuffed it in his mouth. "'S'good," he said in between chews.

I bit into the dark chocolate truffle I chose. A burst of ginger hit my taste buds, and I groaned with pleasure. "My friend is sooo talented."

With that taste of sweetness, I couldn't wait for Nutty to open his gift. The box was bigger than his body, and he shredded the paper with his tiny paws. I helped him lift off the top to reveal a huge stash of a variety of nuts inside of it.

"Oh, boy!" he squeaked. "Just what I wanted!" With his piece of chocolate barely finished, he stuffed two nuts into his mouth. His cheeks bulged out in a comical way, and I couldn't help giving in to a fit of giggles at his ridiculous appearance.

I stood up and crooked a finger at him. "But that's not all. Come see the second part of your gift." I led him into the kitchen where a red-and-white-checkered tablecloth covered my real gift to him. "Go ahead and see what's underneath it."

Nutty pulled off the cloth and marveled at the chest made of ice. It had leaves and nuts of different varieties etched into its surface.

"That's so you have a place to stash them rather than using our oven and any other place in here. The chest will keep them nice and cool so they'll stay fresh much longer," I explained.

He ran his paws over the surface. "I don't know what to say."

Heat invaded my cheeks, and I smiled even bigger. It felt incredible to give something that was unexpected and so appreciated.

I crouched down and leaned closer to him, kissing the top of his head. "Merry Christmas, buddy."

He knocked his forehead against mine and held it there, nuzzling against me. "Thank you."

A knock on the door interrupted our morning. I padded to answer it and found my boyfriend and Rocky standing outside our modest place.

"What are you doing here?" I exclaimed, ushering them inside and out of the cold.

Wyatt swept me into his arms and swung me around. "I couldn't start my day without wishing you your first Merry Christmas."

"Well, Nutty beat you to that," I teased, smooching him on the tip of his nose.

"Oh, I think you can do better than that." He captured

my mouth with his and kissed me until I forgot all about the special day.

Rocky cleared his throat. "Uh, we brought over some breakfast."

Wyatt let me down on my feet. "That's right. I wanna feed my woman, and then all of us are going to take a ride on the snowmobiles. There's a fresh layer of snow I want to put tracks in."

Nutty and I hustled to get ourselves ready. We scarfed down the egg biscuits that the boys had brought with them. Before too long, the four of us took off like rockets to blaze through the wilderness surrounding Holiday Haven.

We rode for over an hour, stopping here and there to take in the natural sights of the area. Although it was too bright for us to see the Northern Lights, somehow it pleased me to know that they were still up there above us, watching and waiting until they could shine in the night sky.

Wyatt brought us back to the overlook he'd taken me to and shown me his bear for the first time. We all dismounted from the fun vehicles and perched on the rock formation looking out over our small town.

My boyfriend reached into one of his side saddlebags and drew out a thermos. "I know you're not a fan of cocoa, but I thought some of us might like a hot drink to warm up."

"I don't know," I said with a wink. "I'm learning to like a lot of new things."

He pulled out a couple of extra cups and poured the steaming drink out for each of us. Raising the thermos top that served as his mug in the air, Wyatt proposed a toast. "To a Humbug holiday!"

"Hear, hear," agreed Rocky.

Nutty and I pressed our small cups together. "Clink," I said with a giggle.

Wyatt made me scoot forward so he could sit behind me.

He drew me closer to him, and I reveled in the warmth of his body. "Do you always run so hot?" I asked, glancing up at him.

He wiggled his eyebrows at me. "So, you think I'm hot?"

I elbowed him for his joke. "Not that kind of hot."

My boyfriend kissed the top of my head. "Yes, that's one of the effects of my bear. Even in the dead of winter, I don't get cold."

"That will definitely come in handy." I snuggled into his embrace and enjoyed the view.

The thought of what he might think of his gift once he saw it warmed me from the inside out.

I DARED to wear something a little silly to Amos's house for our afternoon of fun. Using some felt, hot glue, and some safety pins, I'd managed to turn my red sweater into an ugly Christmas sweater.

"Ta-da!" I sang out when I entered the house. With great care, I placed the wrapped box for Wyatt under the tree.

"What in the world are you wearing?" Vale asked with wide eyes. "Oh, wait. That's what our sugar cookies are based off of."

"Yep," I beamed. "I've always wanted to wear one to a party before. I forgot to suggest that we turn this into an ugly sweater event as well, so I'm cool with being the only one."

Clarence brought me a glass of eggnog. "Next year," he said, clinking his cup against mine. "And be careful. There's a lot of extra nog in there, if you get what I mean."

It didn't take long for everyone to show up. An electric buzz filled the air from all of our excitement. Of course, Wyatt was the last to arrive, and I waited by the door for him.

The second he got there, I greeted him by pointing up at

the branch of mistletoe hung right over the door. "You gotta pay the toll."

"Gladly," he growled like a starving man. Only the shrill whistles and catcalls from our friends stopped us from getting too hot and heavy.

We entered the living room hand in hand. Someone had brought in extra chairs so we all had a place to sit.

"Don't you need to put your gift under the tree?" I asked.

"Nah," he said with a shake of his head. "I think I'll hold onto it for now."

Vale stood up. "Well, since I'm half-elf, I guess I'll help distribute the gifts." She hustled over and started sorting out the presents from under the tree.

Soon, we all had a gift either placed in front of us if it was big or sitting in our laps, except for Vale. She went back over to the tree and found a large gift leaning against the wall nearby.

"Wait. The tag has my name on it," she said.

"Why don't you go first then, Valey," I suggested.

A shy smile spread on her lips. "Okay." Following her own advice, she tore a strip of paper down the middle. "Oh my stars," she exhaled before clawing off the rest of the wrapping.

Rocky chuckled. "That's a marble slab you can use to temper your chocolate on."

The rest of us complimented the big guy on his choice. Tears formed in Vale's eyes, and she immediately rushed over to the rock troll and hugged him about his neck.

"That was very thoughtful. And I will definitely be using this!" She kissed him on the cheek and dashed a tear away. "I think Rocky should go next."

The troll struggled a bit in being careful with his smaller box. Since Vale took a seat next to him, she assisted in getting the present unwrapped.

Rocky held up a box with a picture of an e-reader on it. "What's this?"

"That, my friend, is a device that stores books on it digitally," Clarence exclaimed. "It's rechargeable, and you can load as many books on there as you'd like. I also signed you up for a membership that allows you to read as many books as you want if they're enrolled in the program."

"Oh, that's cool," Rocky exclaimed. "I won't have to crowd my cave with stacks of romance novels anymore."

"Romance novels?" I said a bit louder than I'd meant to.

The troll nodded. "Mm-hmm. Can't get enough of them. I especially like the ones with other supernaturals like us in them. Helps me to believe that I'll find someone to love someday."

Vale leaned against his arm as she helped him open the box. "You will. I know it."

"Thank you, Clarence," Rocky said.

"You're more than welcome," replied the vampire. "And I'm next."

His present was so meticulously wrapped, I knew Vale must have done it. Of course, the rest of us guessed who his Secret Santa was since the half-elf vibrated in her seat while she watched the vampire take off the paper with great care.

"Oh my giddy aunt, how in the world did you get these?" He held up a long paper tube. "These are Christmas crackers, and it's been ages since I got to pop one of them."

He showed us all how to do it, and distributed the lot around the room. I chose to open mine with Wyatt. We both pulled on the ends until it popped open with a slight bang and small goodies spilled out of the paper.

"Ah, I like the color pink," my boyfriend exclaimed, pulling the pink tissue crown apart and placing it on his head. "You get the red one to go with your amazing sweater."

I held up a tiny screwdriver. "Clarence, what am I supposed to do with this?"

He shrugged. "One doesn't question the sanity of what's in the cracker."

"I found a joke in mine," Amos declared. "It asks who is Santa's favorite singer?"

We all thought about the question and offered a couple of different answers, none of which were right.

"It's gotta be Bing Crosby," I insisted. "Who doesn't love the movie *White Christmas*?"

Wyatt raised his hand. "I can't say whether I do or not. Never seen it."

I shrieked in mock horror. "We will have to remedy that right away."

"The answer is Elf-is Presley. Get it?" Amos cackled. "But instead of spelling his name right, it's spelled E-L-F-I-S."

I checked the remnants of my cracker and found my joke. "Ooh, Clarence. This one's for you. What do you get when you cross a snowman with a vampire?"

"I know this one." The pub owner smiled and flashed his fangs. "Frostbite!"

After we all settled down from sharing our terrible but funny jokes, Clarence finished opening the rest of his gift. He held up a golden box from Yuletide Yummies and thanked Vale.

"I hustled some of your cider and your Holid-Ale and used them to make some new goodies. I hope you don't mind. Plus, at the bottom of the box is a tin of mince pies just for you," she explained. "Oh, and I've included a gift card for one box of chocolates every month for a year."

Clarence thanked her for her generosity and offered to share his riches. By the time today was over, I'd be so hopped up on sugar I probably wouldn't sleep for a week.

Amos tore into his present. "I'm tired of waiting," he

groused with a grin. His expression changed to one of awe when he pulled out a small knife. "This is for whittling. It's very fine. Who gave this to me?"

"Yeah, yeah, I did!" Nutty waved his paw in the air. "Thought you'd like that."

"It's very thoughtful, my little friend." Amos beamed at him. "I think you and I had similar thoughts when coming up with what to get each other. Open your gift."

The squirrel tore into his gift with the same enthusiasm he displayed this morning. Clarence helped him remove the top of the box to reveal a gorgeous nutcracker inside. When Nutty took it out, it stood taller than him.

"Now, that's not just for show. I made sure he was good and sturdy. You go ahead and crack your nuts in his jaws," Amos said. "Oh, and I subscribed you to this club that will send you a different box of them to your place every month, too."

Instead of hugging the man who'd made the object, Nutty threw his arms around the nutcracker and squeezed it tight. "I love him. Thank you, Amos."

"You are more than welcome." The smile on the older man's face reassured me that we had picked the right place to hold our small party.

"Well, that just leaves the two of us," said Wyatt. "Although I have to admit, I traded Clarence for your name."

"And I switched with Nutty," I chuckled.

A chorus of *aww* and one distinctive *eww* from Amos rose in the air. I flipped them all off.

"Oh, real nice. And on Christmas Day. What would Santa say?" Amos joked.

Wyatt pulled a small wrapped box from his pocket. The size of it scared me. Sure, I really liked the guy. Maybe even liked him enough to consider the bigger *L* word. But it was way too soon for a piece of jewelry that would fit into a box that size.

My boyfriend ran a finger from the middle of my forehead down to the tip of my nose and squeezed. "Stop freaking out. It's way too early to be thinking thoughts like that."

I blew out a sigh of relief and held out my hands to accept the small package. With trembling fingers, I unwrapped it and clicked open the velvet box.

"Oh my stars, that is gorgeous." I picked up the pendant from inside and let it dangle from the chain.

"The top of that is an opal. It's encased in wood pieces to make it look like the mountains." Wyatt spoke low and steady. "It looks like—"

"The Northern Lights," I finished. "It looks just like the sky that first night you took me for a snowmobile ride."

"The Aurora Borealis for *my* Aurora," he said. "May I put it on you?"

I nodded and turned, pulling my hair back with my hands. With great care, he secured his gift and placed a quick kiss on the back of my neck.

Vale popped out of her seat so she could come over and admire it. "You did good, Wy," she complimented.

"I had help." Wyatt nodded at Amos.

I looked down at the pendant sitting against my chest. "It's so beautiful. I don't know what to say. Except thank you."

He turned me around to face him. "You're more than welcome. I wanted something more special than just one of my carvings."

I tilted my head. "I was thinking the same thing about my gift for you."

He rubbed his hands together with glee. "I can't wait to see what it is." His foot carefully kicked the box at his feet.

Chapter Seven

With childish impatience, Wyatt tore apart the wrapping I'd so carefully placed to his box. He opened the flap and stared into the container.

"I...this is...thank you?" he said, giving me a weak smile.

"You don't even know what it is," I teased, enjoying the first part of my gift.

"I think I must speak for all of us when I repeat what he said. What is it?" Amos asked.

Wyatt pulled out a mason jar of cherries, a few sprigs of rosemary, and other items, spreading them out on the floor.

"Those are all different ingredients that you can use to experiment with. I thought you could try infusing your moonshine with them," I explained.

"Ohhh," he drew out. "That's a really cool idea.

I fanned myself with my hand. "I do get one or two of them once in a while." My spell phone pinged, and I pulled it out of my pocket. "Perfect timing. We're going to need to clear this area in front of us," I instructed.

Clarence and Rocky did as I asked, but Wyatt stood next to me with a puzzled expression on his face. "Why?"

"Because we need to make room for the second part of your present." To hide my anticipatory delight, I replaced the ingredients back in the box and put it on the couch.

The scent of hot cocoa, a wood fire, and cranberries filled the air. Snowflakes that smelled and tasted like peppermint fell around us. A whirlwind of the stuff appeared in the middle of the room, and I backed away with the rest of my friends to give it room.

Clara walked through into Amos's living room. "Well, this is all very cozy."

"Santa's wife is my present?" Wyatt asked in confusion.

The older lady snorted. "I think we're both already taken, young man. No, I'm not your present. But *he* is."

A dark figure walked out of the vortex of snow and stood next to Mrs. Claus. He stood almost as tall as Wyatt although the top of his head was bald except for a small tuft of wispy hair right in the middle.

"Grandpappy?" Wyatt asked in wonder. "Grandpappy!" he shouted, rushing forward and crushing the old man in his arms.

"Wyatt, my boy!" the older gentleman exclaimed, slapping his grandson on the back. "It is so good to see you!"

Clara came over and stood next to me. "Now, that is definitely the right gift. And it wasn't listed anywhere in my husband's books. You did good, kid." She bumped me with her hip.

"I couldn't have done it without you," I admitted. "Thanks for the help."

"For the woman who rebuilt my husband's sleigh? Anytime!" she promised.

Wyatt kept an arm around his grandfather's shoulders. "This here's my Grandpappy, Caleb Berenger." He introduced the other Humbugs to him. "And this is Aurora Hart. I think she's the one responsible for bringing you here."

Wyatt's grandfather extended his hand to me. "My land and stars, you have no idea what a gift you've given to both of us." His Southern accent matched that of his grandson's.

"You're more than welcome, Mr. Berenger," I said, blinking back the tears in my eyes.

The older man cackled. "Now, anyone who's as sweet as you needs to call me Caleb. Or even Grandpappy. And I sure do appreciate that sweater you're wearing." He puffed out his barrel of a chest, showing off the ugly one he had on. "I didn't have time to change before Mrs. Claus here came and explained everything."

"It was my pleasure." The scent of Clara's magic gathered around her. "And we've made sure the rest of your family has special access to the Winternet so that you can keep in better contact with them and not get caught. You may be a permanent resident here, Wyatt, but that doesn't mean you have to lose that which is most precious to you."

"No, ma'am," my boyfriend replied with a wide smile. "I'm pretty sure I've gained much more than I thought I lost." He pulled me closer to him so he had one arm around me and one around his grandfather.

Santa's wife winked at him before stepping back into the maelstrom of her magic. "I hope you all enjoy your holiday. I'll be seeing you soon." The snow sparkled and swirled around her until she disappeared.

"How long do I get you?" Wyatt asked.

"A whole week," Grandpappy replied.

"Good. Maybe you can help me figure out what to do with the rest of Rory's gift to me." Wyatt showed him the contents of the first box.

The rest of the group milled about and got refreshments while admiring each other's gifts. I stuck close to Wyatt but didn't want to bother him too much, wanting him to spend as much time as possible with his grandfather.

"Excuse me one moment, Grandpappy. There's something I need to do," Wyatt said, rising from his place next to his kin.

My boyfriend approached me and cradled my cheek in his large hand. "Thank you doesn't even begin to express what's inside my heart. No one has ever given me a more perfect gift."

I touched the pendant hanging around my neck. "Me either," I managed in a whisper.

He leaned closer and gave me a sweet kiss before embracing me so hard that I almost lost my breath. I smacked him on his back.

"Too...hard..." I struggled.

"Well, what do you expect from a big bear other than a bear hug?" his grandfather joked.

Wyatt leaned down and whispered in my ear, "I'll thank you properly when we're alone later."

Warm shivers ran down my body, and I grinned with goofy elation at him. "Promises, promises," I teased.

Vale and Clarence handed out flutes of champagne to everyone. Amos stepped forward until he stood in the middle.

"I'd like to make a toast." He cleared his throat. "Saying I'm grateful seems too small of a sentiment to capture everything that's in here." He tapped his chest on the left side.

"I feel the exact same way," Wyatt added.

Murmurs of agreement rustled around the group.

Amos continued. "My Mabel was the one who was good with words, so I'll stick with what she would say. To love, to friendship, and to life. May we appreciate and be blessed with all three. Merry Christmas, everybody."

"Merry Christmas," we all repeated, holding our glasses in the air.

We clinked them together, making sure to look each other in the eyes as we cheered together.

My heart felt close to bursting with happiness. Glancing around at my chosen family, I just couldn't hold in all of my excitement and gratitude.

I lifted my glass and beamed at everyone. "And a Happy Humbug Holiday to all of us!"

DEAR READER - THANK you for reading *Sleigh Spells* and the bonus *A Humbug Holiday*! If you're ready for more of Rory and the Humbugs, get ready to read Cheery Charms now!

Read all of the Winter Witches

Read the entire Winter Witches of Holiday Haven Series!

Sleigh Spells by Bella Falls
Reindeer Runes by Danielle Garrett
Holiday Hexes by J. L. Collins
Winter Wishes by Elle Adams
Cocoa Curses by Erin Johnson
Cheery Charms by Bella Falls
Peppermint Pixies by Danielle Garrett
Jolly Jinxes by J. L. Collins
Holiday Hijinks by Elle Adams
Solstice Spirits by Erin Johnson
Merry Mischief by Bella Falls
Evergreen Elves by Danielle Garrett
Icy Illusions by J. L. Collins
Tinsel Trickery by Elle Adams
Mistletoe Mojo by Erin Johnson

All of the stories take place in the same wonderful winterland of Holiday Haven! They can be read and enjoyed in any order!

Join the Coffee Cauldron reader group to get behind-the-scenes info, have a little holiday fun, and of course, join in some fun giveaways! Make it Witchmas all year long!

Also by Bella Falls

Southern Relics Cozy Mysteries

Flea Market Magic

Rags To Witches

Pickup and Pirates

Vintage Vampire

Bargain Haunting

A Southern Charms Cozy Mystery Series

Moonshine & Magic: Book 1

Lemonade & Love Potions: A Cozy Short

Fried Chicken & Fangs: Book 2

Sweet Tea & Spells: Book 3

Barbecue & Brooms: Book 4

Collards & Cauldrons: Book 5

Red Velvet & Reindeer: A Cozy Short

Cornbread & Crossroads: Book 6

Preserves & Premonitions: Book 7

Grits & Ghosts: Book 8 (Coming Soon)

*All audiobooks available are narrated by the wonderful and talented Johanna Parker

For a FREE exclusive copy of the prequel to the Southern Charms series, Chess Pie & Choices, sign up for my newsletter!

Share recipes, talk about Southern Charms and all things cozy mysteries, and connect with me by joining my reader group Southern Charms Cozy Companions!

Hextra Free Stories

Want to read more about your favorite characters? Check out the free "hextra" stories available to all subscribers to my newsletter or members of my reader group Southern Charms Cozy Companions!

Click here to subscribe:

https://books.bookfunnel.com/bellasubscriberhextras

Click here to join:

Southern Charms Cozy Companions

Acknowledgments

I want to thank my fellow Winter Witches authors—Danielle Garrett, J.L. Collins, Elle Adams, and Erin Johnson. This has been a fun world to create with all of you!

About the Author

Bella Falls grew up on the magic of sweet tea, barbecue, and hot and humid Southern days. She met her husband at college over an argument of how to properly pronounce the word *pecan* (for the record, it should be *pea-cawn,* and they taste amazing in a pie). Although she's had the privilege of living all over the States and the world, her heart still beats to the rhythm of the cicadas on a hot summer's evening.

Now, she's taken her love of the South and woven it into a world where magic and mystery aren't the only Charms.

bellafallsbooks.com
contact@bellafallsbooks.com
Bella Falls' Newsletter
Southern Charms Cozy Companions

facebook.com/bellafallsbooks
twitter.com/bellafallsbooks
instagram.com/bellafallsbooks
amazon.com/author/bellafalls
bookbub.com/authors/bella-falls